William Vincent Byars

The Glory of the Garden

And Other Odes, Sonnets and Ballads in Sequence

William Vincent Byars

The Glory of the Garden
And Other Odes, Sonnets and Ballads in Sequence

ISBN/EAN: 9783744784115

Printed in Europe, USA, Canada, Australia, Japan

Cover: Foto ©Andreas Hilbeck / pixelio.de

More available books at **www.hansebooks.com**

THE GLORY OF THE GARDEN

AND OTHER ODES,

SONNETS AND BALLADS

IN SEQUENCE.

WITH A NOTE ON THE RELATIONS OF THE HORATIAN ODE TO THE TUSCAN SONNET.

BY WILLIAM VINCENT BYARS.

"Alles Vergaengliche
Ist nur ein Gleichniss;
Das Unzulaengliche
Hier wird's Ereigniss;
Das Unbeschreibliche
Hier ist es gethan;
Das Ewig-Weibliche
Zieht uns hinan!"

To All Good Women and All Who Love Them!

The Glory of the Garden.

THE light of stars and suns, a wild flower's scent ;
    The night's dim mystery of unending space ;
The first faint flush of morn's most transient grace,
The last blush on the clouds when day has spent
Its lavish wealth of sunset—these were blent
To make the beauty for the soul and face
Of the first woman, born in that fair place
Of paradise, wherefrom so soon she went,
Outcast and banned.   But still, O Mother, we
Of your soul's beauty and your sin are fain !
Though knowledge comes not but at cost of pain,
Yet conquering death through pain each soul shall be
By love made beautiful and strong and free ;
Nor shall the poorest life be lived in vain !

HELEN.

THE glow of sunlight on the morning sea ;
      The play of shadows on the woodland grass ;
The gleam of clouds across the moon that pass ;
The breath of flowers upon the springtime lea—
These bring thy memory, Helen, back to me
And all who seek (is it in vain, alas !)
The gold of sunset from the skies to amass
And buy the knowledge of life's mystery.

Thy magic spell of beauty doth pervade
The earth, the sky, the sea's untrodden ways.
From age to age throughout all change of days,
Enduring and undying, ne'er to fade,
Thy spirit lives in all that heaven has made
And souls of all men still thy beauty sways.

WHITE QUEEN BLANCHE.

An Ode.

WHAT avails the rare scent of a rose in the sun ;
  Of a lily that blooms for an hour and is gone ?
Fair sirs, with your science, you put them to scorn ;
But will ye make me the loom where the lily was spun ?
Where its thread was blent when God said : "Well done !"
Will ye mix me the red of the rose at morn
With perfume that hath lifted a heart forlorn
To the throne of heaven's Highest and Holiest One ?

That white Queen Blanche who was fair for an hour
Is naught now but the scent of a delicate fame ;
But slight not her beauty, my masters, nor shame
The sheen and perfume of the morning flower
When its bloom is a witness of high heaven's power
And its scent gives glory to God's great name !

PANDORA.

THE spirit world is open !   Rise and gaze
     On fragrant morning meadows, wet with dew !
Be still and listen, for all things anew
Speak with a thousand tongues to tell heaven's ways
Of love and light !   Beneath the sun's first rays,
The sweet, small flowers that prayed and hoped and grew
Through all the night, proclaim in scent and hue
A gospel that endures throughout all days.

When first Pandora came on earth she brought
Spirits of beauty, light and truth and grace
To cheer what else had been a cheerless place !
They are hope's messengers whose work is wrought
By all fair things but most by the pure thought
That glows in beauty on a woman's face.

WITCH LILITH.

TRUST not Witch Lilith for her golden hair,
The ivory of her throat or her rose hue,
For she of old twined round the tree that grew
Central in paradise.   With lies most fair,
She works her spell of woe on all who dare
The magic of her eye's most potent blue !
If you but kiss her mouth, her tongue anew
Shall hiss its serpent curse.   Ah, then beware
Her deadly beauty !   But for her no joy
Could end in pain ; no poisons dread and fell,
Would lurk in flowers that lure but to destroy ;
Music could have no discords, love could never cloy,
Nor could an earth where seraph souls might dwell
Be foul with venom of her serpent hell !

MARY OF THE MANGER.

THIS little world swings through unending space,
   A speck of darkness in the luminous night
Which ever and anon flames forth in light
Of radiant spheres, full of heaven's joy and grace ;
And far beyond all these is that void place
Where lost souls grope in awful, blind affright,
Through blackest silence in heaven's pitying sight,
Scorning the light and turning from God's face !

These are the manger's mysteries whose worth
Makes that of motherhood !   Each new-born soul
Has in the endless skies its final goal
Of life that shall endure when stars and earth
And suns and centuries no longer roll
Throughout the sphered eternities of birth !

DELILAH.

A SPELL of death lurks in Delilah's eyes
And the red-golden meshes of her hair
Are woven to make for all men's souls a snare—
A witch's snare of life's most lovely lies.
Her lips with guile of laughter or low sighs,
Woo them whose idle footsteps pass her lair
To enter in and breathe the enchanted air
Which maddens fools and makes as fools the wise.

When one is captive to her, he shall grind
A grist of woe by day and dolorous night.
Shorn of his strength, deprived of heaven's glad light,
Scorned, spat upon, in prison-mills confined,
He lives as one accursed beneath the blight
Of the foul spell that made him weak and blind.

CIRCE.

THERE is a goddess, Circe, whose red wine
Sparkles in beakers in a king's high hall,
Where like a queen she stands to welcome all
Who come, storm-tossed and weary of the brine.
Most fair she stands and with her smile divine,
She charms the wayworn wretch to be her thrall ;
But he who drinks her wine shall find it gall
Nor shall his soul find rest among her swine.

If thou hast eaten moly and dost bear
A sword whose steel is proof against her spell,
Then fear her not.   She has no might to quell
Him whom long pain has taught to do and dare
Whate'er heaven wills.   But watch and be thou ware
When first thy parched lips taste her potions fell !

EURYDICE.

D EAR dream of youth, bright lost Eurydice,
    Seen still in sunlight gleaming on the mere,
The soul that learns of love to cast out fear,
Shall grow with beauty and with truth of thee
Strong in truth's strength and in its beauty free,
Communing with all spirits of that sphere
Where love and hope and faith and truth endear,
Binding all hearts with bonds the soul's eyes see !

But ah, Eurydice, lost love, thy grace
Evanishes with clouds that hide the sun ;
For sea and mere grow gray when day is gone,
And as we turn to look upon thy face,
It fades away into that awful place,
Of dim, vast, shadowy twilight, stern and dun !

PSYCHE.

O F all fair truths of heaven old fables tell
   The surest is that story of a soul ;
A woman's soul that broke from fear's control,
And sought lost hope beyond the gates of hell,
Brave with a love no cowardice could quell
Nor terrors of the gloom turn from its goal ;
And still while time's uncounted ages roll,
She follows hope, the captive of love's spell !

And it is well ; for she who follows hope,
Though Love's feet lead her into darkest night,
Shall surely learn through love her way to grope
To sweeter day, to purer, fairer light
Wherein her soul shall see with clearer sight
Eternal things beyond time's mete and scope !

PENELOPE.

A LOVE there is that burns a sacred fire ;
　　Too pure to wane for change of day or night,
It lightens home with calm, celestial light,
Making the hearth an altar where desire
Consumes as incense to a holier god and higher
Than the blind love of youth !　In Time's despite,
That hallowed flame shines clearer and more bright
When passion fails and all its ardors tire !

One whom long years of struggle had made wise,
To proffered gifts of immortality
Preferred his home and gray Penelope !
Did he not well?　And shall not all our eyes
Strain hard as his toward the home that lies
In some fair land beyond the vast, dim sea ?

THE SYBIL.

OUR souls are little and our lives are mean ;
    We creep and swarm as ants who for a day,
Strive here and there along some dusty way
Until the sunset !   But to souls serene
Of Vala and of Sybil heavens unseen
And vanished centuries in long array
Reveal their truths, their secret thoughts betray,
Until all mysteries that lie between
The two eternities are theirs.   If you have known
Such deep, prophetic voices, if a tone
Of power to call to light the darkest years
Has sounded through the night upon your ears,
Happy are you though you should stand alone,
Bearing men's slights, their coldness and their sneers !

THE VALA.

WITH soul illumined by the boreal light
    That flashes radiant round the Northern pole,
She saw the crashing centuries as they roll
In thunderous music through the dim, vast night.
She saw swift-winged Eternities whose flight
Shames Time to stillness, for their goal
Is the completeness of the immanent Whole—
The everlasting Mind which gives sure sight
To eyes like hers !   Things past and things to be,
Life, Death, Hell, Heaven, Earth, Sky and boundless Sea
To her swift questions gave their sure replies !
Beyond Time's night she saw new worlds arise,
Always enduring !   And with gladdening eyes,
She saw all souls from Fate's sad law set free !

LUCRETIA.

THE blood that stained the chaste Lucretia's breast ;
That mantles now upon a maiden's face
At thought of shame, has in it fullest grace
To make an unclean world at last as blessed
And pure as highest heaven.   The poet's quest,
The prophet's yearning hope for some fair place,
Home of a higher and more holy race,
Though ever still to fiends and fools a jest,
She seals as real with witness of the blood
Which redly flowed upon her breast of snow,
That by such token we may surely know
The sacred worth of perfect womanhood—
Such holy worth as theirs of old who stood
On Calvary's mournful summit, weeping low !

FRANCESCA.

WHAT doth love profit now that thou art blown,
  Francesca, down the roaring winds of hell,
A joyless ghost of sins outworn, whose spell,
Once sweet as life, brings now but bitter moan,
For memory of dead joys, aforetime known ·
In lusty spring of life when it seems well
To put away all thought of darkness fell
That reigns where endless death usurps love's throne !

If as thou sayst (as one who weeps and says)
There is in earth and hell no grief like this,
When hopeless Misery thinks on happier days,
Hast thou done well to tread forbidden ways,
Giving fair heaven for one brief moment's bliss
And thine own soul for one hot, shameful kiss ?

BEATRICE.

A STREAMING glory of heaven's holiest light
    Falls on her brow, and round her gold-bright hair
Truth's halo shines with beams divinely fair
For all whose eyes receive her gift of sight.
Her beauty's glorious sheen gleams through the night
At the pit's mouth to lighten them who dare
The unknown darkness and the night's despair,
Braving hell's hosts alone for love of right !

She is that lady who for love of thee
With seraph-souls on high doth sue for grace.
Kneeling hard by the throne, she makes her plea,
Praying that thou mayest come to that fair place,
Which waits the brave whose eyes at last shall see
The unsullied splendor of Truth's flaming face !

PERDITA.

WHERE the full moon shines on the river's breast
  In celestial splendor of white, pure light,
She lies as asleep in the blue sky's sight
With a face as calm as a child at rest ;
Though her name once fair be now but a jest '
Where the tongues of revel make foul the night,
She drifts with her brow in a glory as bright
As gleams round the haloed heads of the blest !

Is she lost, shut out from the heavens of love,
Where the pure in heart on their harps of gold
Make soft music with meanings manifold?
When shame brings death, is there rescue above?
Was her last cry potent, a prayer to move
The stern law that at last on sin lays hold?

MARY OF SINS.

FROM the wayside's dust, from reek and from slime
     God maketh a man, a maid or a flower,
To endure a year, a day or an hour,
Or to outlast death and all worlds and time !
As from a singer's soul is born a rhyme
Of the glad sun and the sky and the shower,
So by the spirit of God and his power
Was born in the fervent Judean clime,
That fair Mary of Sins from whom were cast
Seven fiends of the Pit by the Master's word ;
Seven sins they were of the gray world's old past,
Of that ancient night where life coldly stirred,
When heaven's fiat lux ! all chaos heard
And God's lightnings flashed through the blackness vast !

MARY OF SORROWS.

NOT in Time's stretch nor out beyond the years
  In the vast void where Time has ceased to be,
Is there a deeper, holier mystery
Than God's deep secret of the bitter tears
Sad mothers still must shed while to his ears
Comes from the cross the everlasting cry :
" Eloi, eloi lama sabachthani ! "
Echoing far out to his remotest spheres !

Mother of sorrows, Mary of the Cross,
Of Calvary's secrets still thy sons are fain !
No tear of thine was ever shed in vain ;
For without tears, love's finest gold were dross,
Since every living soul has birth through pain
And new life comes not but by old life's loss !

HELOISE.

I S not all true love sad, O Heloise !
   A victim garlanded for sacrifice
Who knows not how she may in any wise
Escape the knife that with charmed eye she sees
When with slow hand the careful high-priest frees
Its bright blade from the sheath ?   So were your eyes
Set on your fate when stifling back love's sighs,
You drained life's draught to its most bitter leas !

But though the nun's black veil hides your sad face
To cover all love's sin, through it doth shine
Into time's night a radiance most divine,
A light of heavenly love so full of grace,
It fills and brightens all the void, drear space
Where Death his captive ages doth confine !

NAOMI AND RUTH.

SUBTLE of soul Naomi was, for she in sooth
　　Knew that sweet magic by whose spell a maid,
Though she herself be shamefaced and afraid
In trembling coyness of her unworn youth,
Conquers men's souls as then in very truth
Boaz was won when ere the night could fade,
He measured barley and at parting laid
A kinsman's gift into the arms of Ruth.

In some forgotten life or in some dream,
I saw the waving fields of yellow wheat
Where Ruth, the Gleaner, stood with brown, bare feet ;
And he who saw how white her beauty's gleam
Shone through her tattered dress, might surely deem
A royal robe had been for her most meet!

LAURA.

THE poet learns from all things.   He is taught
     By music of clear waters as they flow
Through sunlit glades in June when whispering low,
They strive to tell him their most tuneful thought
Of the bright seas they seek.   All things are fraught
For him with love and light.   He learns to know
Heaven's secret ways from grace of flowers that grow
In wood and field.   The farthest star had naught
Of mystery for him if he knew a rose
And the neglected grass that rankly grows
On children's graves.   Yet never is he wise
Until a woman's loving soul he knows
And from her beauty learns to read the skies,
As Petrarch learned them from his Laura's eyes.

CECILIA AND ROSSETTI.

HE was but newly dead and had no might
        To make such songs as heaven's sweet poets make
And set to music !   As a child awake,
Lying alone and sleepless in the night,
Stretches its futile hands towards the light,
He cried aloud that soon his heart must break
Unless some spirit deigned for love's dear sake
To give his voice its song, his wings their flight !

Then at his calling fair Cecilia came,
The sweetest singer in the heavenly choir !
Drawn downward to him by his strong desire,
She took his hand, told him his heavenly name,
And as blent strains from one harmonious lyre,
They mounted upward in a singing flame ! *

---

* "And the souls mounting up to God
  Went by her like thin flames !"
                                        Rossetti.

SAPPHO.

THE west wind sighs for Sappho for she lies
    Where cold waves lap her breast and her loose hair
Floats golden with the tide ! Serenely fair
Is her white face, and her deep, azure eyes
Are closed in dreamless sleep ! Never in any wise
Will she weep more. Never again love's care,
Its pain, its grief, its shame will bring despair
To her still breast or wring from her the cries
She set to music of that harp whose strain
First gave to woman's heart a voice and tune !
Suns rise and set ; the pitying crescent moon
Above the summer seas doth wax and wane,
But Sappho wakes not, having of death this boon,
Never to laugh or sigh or sing again !

KATISHA.

IN darkness of the night stood one unknown,
  Lifting a torch to shine for all men's eyes,
With might of a great truth made brave and wise,
He cried aloud :   " Lo God is God alone !
There is no other God upon heaven's throne
Than God the Gracious, who with pitying eyes,
Sees all your pain and hears the wailing cries
You send in vain to your dumb lies of stone ! "

So he cried out ; but they who loved their wrong
Saluted him with louder answering cry :
"Fool and blasphemer, thou shalt surely die ! "
But by Katisha's faith and trust made strong,
He braved alone the fury of the throng
And scorched with torch of flame their fierce-faced lie !

MARY WASHINGTON.

NO man is great whose mother makes him small ;
    No man is small whose mother makes him great ;—
This is a two-fold cord of triple fate ;
Though men be weak or strong, it binds them all ;
The greatest and the least it holds in thrall ;
In good or evil hap, in love or hate,
As banned outlaws or highest chiefs of state,
Men are their mother's sons, whate'er befall !

So Washington, his mother's son, she made
A gentleman, firm, simple, brave and true,
Great for all time because he dared to do
The simple duty conscience on him laid ;
And as new ages give him honors new,
Hers too shall be a fame that will not fade !

NANCY HANKS.

WHEN womanhood upon this woeful earth
　　Bears all its shame, its poverty, its pain,
And meekly ignorant, dares not complain,
But toils in silence from a lowly birth
To a forgotten grave—brave in life's dearth
Of love and joy and counting still for gain
All tears love gives though they be given in vain,
It has in such estate heaven's highest worth.

From such a soul of speechless motherhood
Was Lincoln's patience and his sadness born ;
And when he sealed his life-work with his blood,
She who had lived and died, despised, forlorn,
Bearing men's taunts, or foolish, silent scorn,
A radiant spirit, at his bedside, waiting, stood !

DULCINEA.

THE world were surely worse if Quixote's eyes
    Had been as keen as ours ; for blest is he
Whose vision is too nobly weak to see
The flaws in things beloved.   Love is more wise
Than unbelief that, ever-doubting, tries
All things before it trusts nor dares to be
Wrong for the right's sake, foolish to be free
From supreme folly in unfaith that lies !

Thrice blest is he who loves some shining star,
Who lives his life by its celestial rule ;
Happy though reckoned by all men a fool ;
Thrice happy, though it shines in skies afar
Beyond his sight, while in some shallow pool,
He catches but its faint, reflected light !

THE LADIES OF OLD TIME.

WHO does not love the ladies of old time?
    Their heads erect, their sweet and stately grace,
The mild, seraphic pride illumining each face
Are music to the eyes, such fleet recurrent rhyme
As lute-players make when every string keeps chime
To a pure thought of some bright garden space
Where smell of lilies perfumes all the place
Till memory thrills with odors of heaven's clime.

But they are gone like dew on last year's flowers
That grew in crannies of the crumbling walls
And mouldering stones of those proud, lonely halls
Where once they reigned!   Their lands, their towers,
And greater things than these the years make ours
Whose mothers were their unconsidered thralls!

THE RAGPICKERS.

I SAW three women, haggard, grim and gray,
   Sorting the vilest refuse of the street ;
Searching for life as if life still were sweet,
Despite the anguish of its bitterest day ;
And I was fain to turn my face away
For pain and pity.   At that sight unmeet,
I could have wept that youth should be so fleet
Had not my obdurate heart been moved to pray.

"O God," I said, " make beautiful again
In some fair world, the lives of such as these
Who here on earth in ugliness and pain
Thus work thy will while we who live at ease
Know not what dearth they bear.   If thou dost please,
O God most high, let no soul's life be vain ! "

CATHERINE OF DOUGLAS.

GOD loves the brave.   The hero and the saint
    Have wrought his will because they dared to be
True to themselves and from the falsehood free
That fawns and lies and truckles till the taint
Of cowardice its ashen hue doth paint   ,
On the fair rose of courage.   O friends, trust me !
The highest heaven of heavens they shall not see
Whose knees are feeble and whose hearts are faint !

Love truth, love right and let all those who list
Be great by might of lies and power of gold !
If, at the midnight hour, your lips are kissed
By seraph-flames of truth and light, be bold
To stand at mid-day as once stood old
Catherine of Douglas with her broken wrist !

CLEOPATRA.

A SINGLE blood-drop on her bosom's snow
    Proclaims the flaw at which her life found vent—
Whence naked, trembling and ashamed, there went
A soul of many names and centuries of woe !
Helen she was and Sappho !   None may know
Her transmutations or the ages spent
In pain of passion ere the spirit pent
In Cleopatra's breast ebbed wan and slow
Beneath the asp's fell fang.   Beware the snake !
For this fair lotus-bloom, the perfumed dower
Of passionate beauty, works a spell of power,
With fleet, Nilotic visions that forsake
Dreamers who trust them, leaving them to wake
Stung by the asp that lurks below the flower !

CLOTHO.

THE wild crab's odorous wealth of snowy bloom,
   Is it not hope of everlasting life?
And is not hope a flowering memory, rife
With mysteries of past birth?   Time's never ceasing loom
Still weaves day's brightest light into night's gloom
For resurrection robes.   White lilies grow
On graves in triumph over death below,
And Hope's most hallowed altar is the tomb.

The wreath of wild-crab flowers in Clotho's hair,
Is it not sweet to smell?   And will not she
Come at your call as still she comes to me
When after night and winter, Spring makes fair
The world with fragrant memories of the rare,
Sweet, vanished days we nevermore shall see?

ATROPOS.

THE forests are a flame of gold and red ;
   The light breeze plays with slowly falling leaves ;
It is the time of Atropos and garnered sheaves ;
Of ripened deeds and of the long-drawn thread
That waits the shears.   For Hope at last has wed
Fruition, and thereby at last conceives
Fate, whereat the Goddess smiles or grieves
When to its end the careworn year has sped !

The flower enfolds the fruit, the fruit, the seed
Of the new life and never-ending birth,
That gives to meanest things new truth, sure worth
And nobler grace.   When Atropos gives heed,
Fair flowers may spring from e'en the vilest weed
That now deforms waste places of the earth !

NEMESIS.

A LL things with everlasting life are fraught ;
  Nothing in earth or sky can cease or fail ;
Whether men laugh or sigh or bless or rail,
No man escapes himself.   Each act, each thought,
Into his soul's eternity is wrought ;   ·
So shall each suffer all his own loved crime
While Time endures and then beyond all Time,
Until Eternity has come to naught !

This is the changeless law !   Let all beware
Nemesis and the serpent twining in her hair.
She is the Unforgetting !   When she sees
The despot writhe in hell, she will not spare !
For all who suffer wrong in silence—these
Have friends in her and the Eumenides !

PROSERPINE.

THE sun still shines though we may think it set ;
    The night is but a shadow on our eyes ;
The hosts of heaven possess the midday skies,
All radiant still, howe'er we may forget
The splendor of their beauty.   Never yet
Has light failed or has life in any wise
Ceased for the lapse of years and changing guise
Of mutable time.   Then let no vain regret
Mar the dear memory of the blessed dead !
For they beyond the sunset and the West
By the sweet Queen of Sleep and Dreams are led
To fairer lives wherein no pain, no dread
Mars the deep calm of that eternal quest
Through which each finds at last what he loves best !

HAGAR.

L EANING her weary head upon her hand,
 She sat beneath the palm tree's scanty shade,
Weeping and desolate !   Rejected and betrayed,
Driven out into the desert's waste of sand,
She faints beneath the heat of that strange land,
With never hope to cheer or love to aid
Her failing feet !   So ever weeps the maid
Who for an unmeet love is scorned and banned.

But as she wept forlorn, the hard, bright sky
Thundered with mighty voice Fate's first, great law
Whereby the curse of her sad motherhood
Shall be on all who drive her forth to die !
In wonder then she raised her eyes and saw
That there hardby, heaven's highest angel stood !

RACHEL.

B Y Haran's well, seven nodding palm trees grow.
    At eve their green against heaven's deepening blue
Is sweet to tired eyes as falling dew
After the noon-day heat.   Calmly and slow
The tinkling sheep-bell sounds, and soon the low,
Soft music of the shepherd's shawm will woo
The desert maid to love more warmly true
Than outworn hearts of later years can know.

True love is goodly though akin to pain,
Sweeter than all things, even than death or sleep ;
And he who truly loves will count it gain,
Though for love's sake, his eyes may not refrain
From overflow.   As when among her sheep,
Jacob kissed Rachel and was fain to weep !

DIANA, THE HUNTRESS.

A LL things are rife with unfulfilled desire.
  What seeks Diana on the hills at night
When all the air gleams rhythmically bright
With thrill of moonbeams, rare as if a choir
Sang some sweet tune to love's harmonious lyre?
What seek the blooming orchards, clothed in white,
When May has come and all the world is dight
In beauty and unfolding flowers aspire
In odorous prayer for fruit?   What mystery lies
Below the glittering surface of the sea
At night when all its mighty floods arise,
Shackled by moonbeams, struggling to be free?
Who knows the answer, let him say for me
What seeks the huntress of the seas and skies.

THE WOMAN OF SAMARIA.

THROUGH all the world, heaven's angels walk obscure
    With radiance hidden from our darkened eyes
By forms of humblest clay whose mean disguise
May veil celestial light more rare and pure
Than we with purblind sight could dare endure.
Lo, past your door the way of all these lies !
Most blest are you when one the latchet tries
And enters in !   For your reward is sure
If you but give a single, cooling draught,
Such as from Jacob's well the woman drew
When from her cup the Galilean quaffed !
For ever still he comes on earth anew—
(That peasant God at whom a mad world laughed !)
And he may come, perchance this day, to you !

THE FIVE WISE VIRGINS.

TO-DAY, perchance, some Thought may come to you,
    Fraught with the glory radiant round heaven's throne ;
Or else a still small voice of music and a tone
Of love caught from clear harps of those, the chosen few,
The very chief of cherubim, who view
The face of God.   If such an angel came unknown,
In humble guise of earth, would your soul own
His kinship?   Would you count his message true ?

Fair were the Five Wise Virgins and most fair
Their white robes shone with their five lamps alight ;
Fragrant the bridal chaplets in their hair
And sweet their choral songs.   None might compare
With them in virgin grace—so clear and bright,
Their lamps and faces shone that wedding night.

MARY OF BETHANY.

CONSIDER the lilies ! Are they not more wise
    Because they live all cumberless and free,
Giving the sky their worship, even as she
Who with deep prayer for knowledge in her eyes
Sat at Christ's feet and drank in his replies,
With soul athirst for that great mystery
Of everlasting life ?   So shall she be
Greater than all who dare not trust the skies.

I learned it from the hedge-rose in the spring
That fear is foolish and a wasteful thing.
Is not the wild phlox by the stream more fair
Because it breathes its odors on the air,
Taking no thought for what next year may bring,
With soul unvext by aught of fear or care !

MARTHA.

A LAS, for all who lead blind, burdened lives,
      Weary at morn with work of yesterday,
With lame feet struggling on a stony way
From birth to grave !   Bound in the gyves
Of circumstances, awed by the whip that drives
Doubt's slaves, the thralls of care grow gray
Even in green youth because they say heaven nay,
And strive forever as the coward strives !

What shall they win who lose the better part,
Yet serve the worse with careful, constant heart,
As Martha served, though truth she could not see ?
Humble though their reward may be and low,
Shall they not rest at last and surely know
All mysteries that skies and stars can show ?

THE VALKYRIES.

THROUGH endless depths of sky freed spirits float !
  Through miles on miles of never-ceasing blue
Do mounting souls their upward way pursue,
Until this world is but a shining mote !
Above earth's highest peaks of snow they float ;
Above green, flowering isles most fair to view,
In sunlit, smiling seas, they pause anew,
Aloof from life, from all its strife remote !

For o'er the world as o'er a battle-plain,
Float the Valkyries, choosers of the slain ;
Each silver cloud, each luminous fleece of gray,
Is a swan-maid who bears a soul away
To fair Valhalla where all loss is gain ;
Where strife and darkness end in life and day !

TITANIA.

WHERE spirits wander through a starlit land,
    Titania reigns, a queen of elves and dreams ;
Her robes are of the full moon's brightest beams
Woven with the sumac's scarlet.   In her hand
She holds fair Memory's wonder-working wand,
Wrought of the sunset's lingering, golden gleams,
And jewelled bright with moonlit spray from streams
Whose cascades shine and sing at her command.

Wise are all mortals loved of her, for they
Can hear the silver chime when blue bells ring
And know the tune with which each growing thing
In wood and field keeps time to coming day
And the first strains of sunrise, when the gray
Of skies empearled grows bright and glad larks sing !

THE LORELEY.

TALL, white cliffs gleam, all radiant with red gold
Till the bent stream burns bright with wedded hues
Of sky and foliage, blent with spell that woos
The soul to dreams.   The year grows sad and old ;
The fire about its heart will soon grow cold,
And soon its tears for all its glad days spent,
Will turn to gray the glowing colors, lent
By earth and sky whose hues these depths enfold !

Under the surface of the mirrored skies
In the deep stream, a land of wonder lies ;
And all its mysteries the Loreley knows !
She calls the fisher-boy and joyfully he goes
Down to dark depths from which he ne'er shall rise ;
And on, forever on, the sparkling current flows !

VIVIA PERPETUA.

"ALAS, poor fool!" the pitying praetor said,
    " If you will die, your blood is not on me!
Cry but 'All hail to Caesar!' and go free;
Pour but one cup of wine, bow your proud head,
And you shall live! I tell you, the pale dead
Stray through black night aghast, as you shall be
Unless to Caesar's power you bend the knee
And save your soul from hell's marsh, vast and dread!"

" Nay, my good lord, it is not hard to die!
Bid your slaves strike and make an end of pain!"
So Vivia said! And so she died for truth
That she might live in an unfading youth
With mighty angels of the upper sky
Who teach earth's slaves and saints that death is gain!

THE WITCH OF ENDOR.

S H E drew aside the curtain of the deep
　　And gazed into the void whose twilight veil
Hides worlds destroyed and all weak lives that fail—
(The uncertain souls who choose to die and sleep!)
With straining ears she heard vague spirits peep
And mutter low as the forbidden wail
Of some fell fiend, self-tortured, dared assail
The silence all dead souls are fain to keep!

Lo, when the prophet came from that dim place,
With hoary hair, dishevelled, and fixed gaze
A ghost unlaid, reluctant to her call,
She shrieked aloud! For gory, stern and tall,
The lost and ruined soul of unslain Saul
Came too and stood all grim before her face!

QUEEN MAB.

TO make Queen Mab the faint scent of a rose
　　Was blent with flame and the white, floating reek
The sun shines through above some crystal creek
Whose stream to sparkling seas of Elfland flows.
In that strange land a tree of wonder grows
And he who kisses thrice Mab's lips and cheek
Shall eat its fruit and learn the truth to speak
And know deep lore no other mortal knows !

Who kisses thrice Mab's lips shall learn to sing
Day's meaning and the secrets of the night !
Her lover he shall be and fairies bright
Will hover round him on moon-silvered wing !
And he shall hear the smitten gold chords ring
When stars at evening tune their harps of light !

ISIS.

U NSEEN, unknown, unworshipped, Isis stands
    Beside Life's loom, behind the future's veil ;
With head bowed low and face divinely pale,
She plies the shuttle with unceasing hands,
Weaving into her web the three-fold strands
Spun by Time's bondmaid hours.   For lives that fail
Or souls that thrive, her labor shall avail
In every age throughout all days and lands !

She weaves fair garments of fine silken flame
And clothes therewith earth's ransomed slaves, set free
From bonds of blind despair and ancient shame !
Three-fold the thread, three-fold the web shall be,
And Isis three-fold.   Death is here her name,
But in the skies they call her Liberty !

THE WIDOW AND HER MITE.

SHE gave more than they all for with her mite,
　　She gave her soul that heaven might make it one
With strength and splendor of the midday sun
And with calm glory of blue skies at night,
When far beyond the scope of straining sight,
In other heavens of beauty, seen by none,
Star-beams and sun-rays are together spun
To make truth's halo of celestial light !

She who gives all, shall have all she loves best !
Into her soul the gracious heavens shall pour
Treasures of light from their unmeasured store ;
The Pleiades seven shall shine to make her blest
And their sweet influences at her behest
Shall wait as handmaids round about her door !

THE SIRENS.

I KNOW a green isle where blue, shining seas
  Gleam bright as they break in foam on white sands !
I dream of clear lakes with moon-flooded strands ;
With bold, jutting highlands and flowering trees ;
My soul is beguiled by soft, humming bees ;
By smell of sweet scents from magical lands ;
By music of sirens whose outstretched hands
Call and enthrall me ! Yea these (more than these !)
Call me away from the roar of the street !
With songs enthralling, enchantingly sweet,
They call me away to islands of green
In seas by mortals unsailed and unseen !
From the madding rush and roar of the street,
They call me away to islands of green !

CECILIA IN HEAVEN.

AROUND Cecilia in white, shining stoles,
  Sweet singers kneel to learn heaven's poesy !
Through all blest years of their eternity,
Crowned with high knowledge in fair aureoles
Of golden light, these once sad, burdened souls
Learn gladness now !   From life's most central tree,
They pluck sweet fruit, and by the crystal sea,
Strange music lulls them as the clear tide rolls
From the far shores of time !   Lo, these are they
Of every land and nation on the earth,
Whom tribulation raised to nobler worth !
They sigh no more, for God has wiped away
Their tears !   Their night has passed !   In this new day,
They rise always from birth to higher birth !

THAIS.

THROUGH war's wild clamor, through bloodshed and flame,
The victor's way is ! Who wins the world's throne,
The love of Thais shall be his alone ;
The white arms of Thais (the conqueror's fame,
The laurel undying, a glorious name !)
The bright charms of Thais all are his own !
By might he prevaileth ! Let stricken slaves groan !
For he that faileth—to him is the shame !

Where shields are ringing and sharp darts are hurled ;
Where arrows sing shrill as they cleave the air,
The hero's way is who would win the fair !
Who would woo bright Thais when flags are furled,
Must smite earth's weaklings, nor pity nor spare
For cries or groans till he masters the world !

VENUS OF THE HORSELBERG.

IN a dream-born world on a gleaming throne
  Of tourmaline and chrysolite most fair,
Queen Venus sits and combs her golden hair,
Unseen of all men save of them alone
She chooses in fresh youth to be her own.
For them she weaves a magic three-fold snare,
Spun from desire, delight and fell despair,
To draw them to her hell !   All bright things fl·wn
Of all dead worlds obey her voice and spell.
A queen of sated joys and unfulfilled delight,
She reigns supreme in an enchanted night
Where all vain visions of false beauty dwell,
Floating forever in pale, golden light
That glows around her in her shadowy hell !

THE MERMAIDS AND THE LOTOS EATER.

P ALE, fair-haired and still, a mariner lies
   In a crystal cave in blue depths below
The pearl-strewn sea-reefs where red corals grow !
Mermaidens at morn with wondering eyes
Gaze on his sad beauty and give him sighs.
Forever and ever the tides shall flow,
But he shall never awaken or know
The glad, bright day and the light of the skies !

He ate the sweet lotos : he dreamed bright dreams
Of a higher life and a golden quest
For islands of beauty beyond the west !
He dreams no longer !   Most blessed he seems
As he lies at last in fulness of rest
Where pale, azure light through blue crystal gleams !

EVANGELINE AT PRAYER.

SWEET saint, I see you kneel with upturned face
 Before the altar where the light streams faint
Through high rose-windows whose blent colors paint
Upon your brow a glow that seems the grace
Of that remote, unseen, long-hoped-for place
Where all who pray and strive and do not faint,
Shall meet at last, freed from the earthly taint
That gives me shame as in this holy place
I watch your prayers ! In other, higher airs,
Evangeline, may I kneel down and learn
The heavenly secrets I would fain make mine ;
But now the very thought of them would burn
My soul with fire such as waits him who dares
Mock at your worship, blest Evangeline !

SARAH DRUMMOND.

THROUGH Time's blind night, the ages grope their way !
   With halting feet, slow-moving, still they crawl
Forever on, unseen, unknown of all
Save of high souls whose eyes can see the day
Though it be midnight and all others say
No sun shall rise !   No darkness shall enthrall,
Nor shackles bind, nor fear nor fate appall,
Nor ancient precedents in grim array
Turn them whom heaven appoints to lead their kind
To higher life through fuller liberty !
Though others see not, some there still shall be
Whose gaze prophetic darkness will not blind !
As Sarah Drummond saw, they still shall see
The soul's clear dawn, the sunrise of the mind !

THE KING'S DAUGHTER.

A MINSTREL loved the daughter of a king
 In that far land where souls are bought for hire ;
No poet there dares sing or tune his lyre,
For men wax fat nor suffer bards to sing,
Lest song should stir their sluggish hearts and bring
Such shame as bids awakened souls aspire
And seek the heavens as mounting larks rise higher
In fair spring skies because they dare to sing !

" Nay, nay, I cannot stay," the minstrel said ;
" I love no land of pampered, fawning slaves.
Better the heaving sea's deep, sunless caves
Where cold, dark graves hold many a freeman dead !
Nay, nay, at morning gray or evening red,
Better for me the sea's free, foaming waves ! "

EMPUSA.

HAVE you not known Empusa?   It is she
   Who bore earth's little, strutting lords—who guides
The horse on which the haughty beggar rides.
All they are born of her who strive to be
Great at the cost of men of less degree ;
For of scorched imps who suckle her shrunk sides
She maketh tyrants and her spell abides
On all who struggle for earth's mastery.

He who drives slaves with whip or nod or tongue
Is spawn of hers, and from her loins are sprung
The slimy brood who flatter, fawn and crawl
For place and power, that they may hold in thrall
The helpless of the earth.   She breeds them all !
And for their sake and hers, this song is sung !

THE MAID OF MOY MELL.

A Ballad.

THOUGH Coran, the druid, may mutter his spell,
    The soul of Prince Connla shall never be free !
From the bleak heights of Usna, he looks o'er the sea
To the land of the West where the Shean folk dwell ;
Ah, vain is gray Coran's black art and his spell,
For the wierd of his own soul Prince Connla shall dree !
Ne'er again a spear-wielder in fight will he be,
For he hears the soft call of the Maid of Moy Mell !

Far, far to the West lies the glittering plain,
The Land of Immortals, where sorrow and pain
Come never to them whom the Shean folk save ;
And when their swift curragh comes over the wave,
The voice of the druid shall be all in vain,
For the vast, awful ocean Prince Connla will brave !

THE BEAN-SHEE'S GIFTS.

B RAVE Carroll had danced with the Bean-Shee
    Who gave him greatness and glory and gold,
And smiled as he clutched them with eager hold,
Knowing nought of fell secrets of gramarie !
By her spell from moments thirty and three,
She wrought him the years of his power and told
Piece by piece the tale of the fairy gold
For which he had sold her his liberty !

Brave Carroll awoke when the years were sped,
In a deep, foul cave where the grim, gray light
Made visible through the horrible night
The ghastly phantom to whom he was wed ;
" Lo, I " she said, " am your heart's delight !
We will sleep this night with the sheeted dead ! "

THEKLA LISTENING TO PAUL.

H E spoke with tongue of angels, and the tone
    Rose clear and free as morning carols, sung
In heavenly streets by harpers glad and young,
When a new savior comes to earth unknown,
To follow Christ and walk, unhelped, alone,
That strait, rough way where every heart is wrung
By pain of higher birth.   The listeners hung
With souls enraptured, rising to heaven's throne,
On the strong pinions of that mighty Word.
He told of that high love which purifies
True hearts until the pain of sacrifice
Raises the soul above.   As Thekla heard,
An unknown life deep in her being stirred
And strange, new, holy tears flowed from her eyes.

HERO'S LAST NIGHT.

S HE listened to the wild gale hissing shrill
    Around her tower, as when lost spirits wail
Far in dark depths profound, where shadows pale
Are driven by power of that dread Evil Will
Which wreaks its hate on souls it can not kill
And the sad dead with torture doth assail !
So shrieked the blast, so did the storm prevail,
When Hero looked at eve to the far hill,
Across the foaming wave, where stripped to swim,
By love made brave, Leander stood with gaze
Fixed on her tower as she stretched hands to him !

*   *   *

At morn when in the sky the sun rose dim,
They lay as all must lie whom Love betrays,
Stark on the sands, veiled by the gray, bleak haze !

CECILIA AND AZRAEL.

B ESIDE the tree of life, Cecilia played
    A tune of love upon her harp of gold ;
A psalm which all death's mystery did enfold ;
(It was a lullaby pale Azrael made !)
It told of fields where lilies never fade
Though children pluck all their two hands can hold ;
Where youth and roses ne'er grow dull and old ;
Where death is higher life and undismayed,
Life shall receive Death's loving kiss of peace !
She sang in heaven.   On earth it seemed a voice
Bidding the city's poor, pale children rise
To lands where flowers and sunshine never cease ;
Where earth's sad weaklings shall in love rejoice
Raised high above all pain in glad, bright skies !

HELEN OF THE CUP.

H E thought on shame of his blind, fevered days ;
   On high and noble deeds he ne'er had done ;
On craven stooping that he dared not shun ;
On coward groping in dark, crooked ways,
And on base acts whereby he got men's praise,
Till the hot brine of tears did overrun
His burning eyes !   Then came that gracious one,
The Argive Helen whom a beggar's lays
Make dear to all men !   In a golden bowl,
She mixed a draught cf wondrous, magic might,
The sweet nepenthe which can raise the soul
To higher things.   And as he drank, his sight
Had strength to pierce the mists of his life's night
And view the splendors of its final goal !

AURORA.

D AY breaks ! Through soft, gray skies the new dawn thrills,
    As music thrills the heart when some loved tune
Wakes a sad soul to joy ! Day breaks and soon
The splendid sun will rise o'er far, blue hills
And its glad light will glitter on bright rills
Through all the land. Day breaks and the pale moon
Gleams wan for grief that night must pass so soon.
The world awakes ! With light the dim sky fills,
As fair Aurora comes with all her train !
Day breaks, Love's soul awakes and all life's pain
Shall pass with grim, gray shadows of the night ;
For all night's loss and fears morn shall requite ;
And every soul that, groping sought the light,
In this new day, its full desire shall gain !

NOURMAHAL.

IN Jamshyd's courts the bramble chokes the rose ;
    And Jamshyd's sword is eaten with red rust ;
The tower of strength whereon he set his trust
Is fallen so low that the foul ragweed grows
On yon cap-stone of pride that dared oppose
The noonday sky !   And this base dust
We tread is Jamshyd's self who had such lust
Of power and praise !   But still the Tigris flows
Beneath blue skies ; and thou, my Nourmahal.
Dost walk with me through this fair garden's ways,
Beside the stream, singing the clear, sweet lays
Through which the soul of Hafiz shall enthrall
The souls of lovers till earth's latest days
When men forget to sing and heaven's stars fall !

RAN, THE QUEEN OF STORMS.

THE black ship staggered and reeled in the sea,
  With cracking timbers and wild-flapping sail ;
For lost souls of dark Nostrand rode on the gale—
(Ah, woeful the shrieks of lost souls must be !)
In the train of fierce Ran who sets them free
When her hoar waves roar and brave men grow pale
To hear the banned ghosts who gibber and wail
When the dread Storm-Queen sways the raging sea !

The black ship sank but Jarl Hakon stood fast
While the flaming lightning flashed in his face !
Ran's ghosts shrieked loud but he kept his place
At the helm of the dragon-ship to the last ;
And hurling his glove at the blackness vast,
He died a true son of his viking race !

FATA MORGANA.

B LEST is the fay, Morgana, who can cheat
   With dreams of cool, sweet springs and meadows fair,
Our desert days of thirst and parched despair !
Fierce glowed the blaze of dread Sahara's heat ;
The deadly noon's red rays accurst, did beat
Full on the wanderer's head with hateful glare ;
Yet hope led still and gave him heart to bear
The pain of cruel ways that scorched his feet !

But when at length he sank and cried for rest,
She raised before his set and glazing eyes
Bright dreams of peace ! and, mirrored in the skies,
She showed the dear-loved home of his long quest,
Where now beside cool streams at last he lies
With all fair, noble souls his soul loved best !

CECILIA AND ISRAFEL.

C ECILIA'S soul is filled with holy peace,
    But Israfel sings not except in pain
Of love that counts as nothing all its gain,
Striving forever, having no might to cease
From prayers for light, and finding no release
From labor, day or night !   And not in vain
He seeks, for they that seek shall gain
From pain of struggle heaven's most potent peace !
They who find peace shall play their music well
On lute or harp, on psaltery or flute !
Most blest is peace and blest are they who dwell
Where songs of hope and love are never mute ;
Where sweet Cecilia sings to that strange lute
Whose strings are the heart-strings of Israfel !

ALCESTIS.

I HOLD in hand two rounded, golden seed ;
A nettle one will make and one a rose !
This is Fate's mystery and no man knows
Science so high that he for me can read
The riddle of these little, golden seed.
From one, Hate's foul and stinging blind-weed grows ;
From one true Love's most fragrant, luminous rose.
So shall each soul inherit its own deed !

This is Fate's law, but ever blest is she,
Like true Alcestis, who can conquer Fate
By might of love that ransoms and sets free
Earth's creeping slaves from shackling deeds of hate,
And that blind chance of dim, ancestral date,
Which breaks Love's law and makes Fate's mystery !

ARACHNE.

WORK now, for night will come and day fades fast !
   Work well, for work is life and hope and peace !
They who work well find strength that shall not cease
For time or change, but time it shall outlast,
Gaining each day from struggle of its past,
New hope, new sight and the eternal peace
They gain who gain at last their sure release
From power of lies that are hell's fiends outcast !

Look how Arachne casts her thin, gray thread
From here to there, from now to yesterday,
That she may win to-morrow ! Do thou spin
As she ! So daily shall thy work be sped
By sorrow as by joy, and thy sure way
Shall lead thee where thy soul its hope shall win !

VENUS LUCIFERENS.

WITH dazzled eyes, worn by the glare of day,
  He turned for peace to calm, cool depths of night,
Where the true evening star rose on his sight,
Shining from far, with tender healing ray,
Through fair, blue skies whose vapors, silvery gray,
Floated in slender wreaths of misty light.
So once again he learned to see aright
And that sweet star taught his sick soul to pray.

Who learns to pray, the stars will make him wise
With night's sweet influence and that mystery deep
Whose secret all heaven's shining stars do keep !
Sweet are gray, silvery mists to tired eyes
And sweet is night that brings the worn soul sleep,
But sweeter still is light from night's deep skies !

ALCESTIS BROUGHT BACK.

A LL we have done and suffered, seen and thought
    Death shall interpret.   This brief life of earth
Must make itself a new and perfect birth,
And be again in warp and woof rewrought.
So do we make our fate !   For death is fraught
With lasting meaning and eternal worth,
Or else with poverty and such sad dearth
Of that high knowledge endless life has taught,
As makes men beggars on heaven's streets of gold.
This is a secret true Alcestis told,
Returning from the land of shadows gray :—
A moment's life eternity doth hold ;
For ere to-morrow can its debt repay,
To-day must borrow all from yesterday !

MORGANA IN AVALON.

H E came at last, worn, faint and stricken sore
    To Avalon where fragrant heartsease grows
Wild through the meadows ; where at twilight's close,
Fair maids sing choral songs full of the lore
Wise spirits of the moon knew, long before
The elves taught men to sing.   There no wind blows
O'er plains of asphodel where sparkling flows
Youth's fount that turns all locks with age grown hoar
Again to the fair hues of golden spring.

Morgana there will teach the weak and dumb
All those high songs they had no art to sing
On earth where speech is a poor, crippled thing.
There life's completeness equals hope's full sum
And there all failing souls at last shall come !

THE NAIAD.

FAR in deep woods, a sparkling stream flows clear
   And pure as starlit heavens, or as the eyes
Of some true-hearted maid not yet grown wise
Through pain of love that mars life's hope with fear.
It is most sweet, when June makes glad the year
With smell of opening flowers and rose-hued skies,
To sit at sunset where bright dragon-flies
Flash on bejewelled wing now there, now here,
Above the stream ! For they are each a thought
Of music, born of that low evening song
The Naiad sings as her soul flows along
The sweet-toned stream whose voice so oft has brought
Heaven's peace and hope to him who here has sought
Rest for a soul grown weary of earth's wrong !

GODIVA.

THERE is an awful and most holy mystery
    Of love and life, of death and change and birth ;
Of law so potent that it sways the earth ;
Of Fate that rules the waters of the sea ;
That maketh hell and heaven by its decree ;
That raiseth lowest things to highest worth,
Giving for darkened emptiness and dearth
Of primal night, that glorious life to be
When all things are made perfect !   'Tis the pain
Of truth and beauty, stripped for sacrifice
By love more strong than shame !   And he whose eyes
That sacred mystery would dare profane,
Deeming such love an idle thing and vain,
Shall wander blind and shameful till he dies !

A RUNE OF THE NORNS.

W HO drinks from Mimir's well shall know the sky,
⠀⠀⠀The earth and all the secrets of the sea,
And hell.⠀Below the roots of that great tree,
The world-ash Iggdrasill, he shall descry
What others think not of !⠀Nor from his eye
Shall Odin's lore be hid ?⠀(Why tempt ye me ?
Witoth er'nn etha what ?)⠀But he shall be
Half blinded by the draught lest he should die !

Know ye not yet what means the Vala's lay ?
Why laughed the Norns, those sisters wierd and gray,
When Odin pawned the better of his eyes
And quaffed the cup that made him sad and wise ?
Have you not learned it yet, to-day or yesterday,
This rune that to your questioning replies ?

THE BEGGAR MAID.

S HE was most fair because her soul was pure !
    Most good to view is that white saintly rose
Whose untouched heart at morn but faintly glows
With blush of dew-wet red.   Its spell is sure.
Its charm of potent magic shall endure
While men love beauty—while the rare perfume
Of fair-souled chastity in virgin bloom
Has strength and power above art's cunning lure !

Her soul was like a flower.   Her face that day
Shone with the morning grace whereby far hills
Are made most fair when dawn's calm star's last ray
Gives place to sunrise and the glad light thrills
To the world's heart.   Thus she with downcast eyes,
Stood all abashed before Cophetuay !

OPHELIA.

SOME souls are like the still blue of the sky
    In a clear pool at morn, fulfilled and blent
With hues of tender green from willows, bent
To view that mirrored heaven and mayhap sigh
For their own earthliness.   Though far and high
The deep empyrean lies, its full intent
Of peace and calm to the fair pool is lent
While undisturbed and still its waters lie !

So was Ophelia's soul most pure and fair
Before sad love wrought madness.   So the stone
By the rude hand of thoughtless wanton thrown,
Degrades the pool to earth.   The sky no more is there,
All heaven's bright hues have faded into air,
And peace and beauty have together flown.

MARY AT THE TOMB.

W HEN Mary came before the night was sped—
       (Who seeketh truth must seek it in the night !)
She found the sepulchre deserted quite ;
But lingering still until the sky grew red
With sunrise, at the feet and at the head
Where Christ had lain, she saw two souls of light
Whose faces shone intolerably bright
With meaning of Truth's rising from the dead !

And so she learned where buried hope had lain
That ere truth triumphs, it must surely die !
Each new-born falsehood has its three days' reign
And for three days new truth must buried lie ;
Men ne'er receive it till they crucify,
But ever is their crucifixion vain !

JOAN OF ARC.

S TRAIT is the gate and rough the way !   Take heed
   If you have ailing feet and feeble soul,
Before you try the path to truth's high goal !
For to cross, stake or scaffold it may lead,
And if your heart should fail you at your need,
Then heaven were mocked.   Shall they who dare enroll
As freedom's vansmen, grudge or spare the dole
Of martyr blood that fructifies truth's seed?

Lo, if you shrink and quake, heaven gives you shame
To see earth's weakest bear the stake and flame,
Daring oppression's worst to make man free !
So by truth's might, the right shall ever be
More strong than strength and so in freedom's name
Shall weakness wrest from wrong the victory !

THE DRYAD OF BANDUSIA.

WHERE sweet Bandusia's limpid waters glide
    The poet dreamed beneath the fair-spread oak,
Hearing strange secrets as the dryad spoke,
Whispering the fountain nymph close at her side,
As they twain listened to the sparkling tide,
Prattling its summer song.   No rude sound broke
His dream of beauty as those fairy folk
Taught him the art his highest art to hide.

As the oak's rustle and the fount's low tune
Told him that strength must have a soul of grace
In every work Time's touch shall not erase,
The sunlit fields were glistening with high noon.
And all the woods were sweet with breath of June,
But sweeter, brighter shone the dryad's face.

PHILOMELA.

A SOUL of tuneful sweetness doth prevail
   Throughout heaven's dream-filled depths of starlit blue !
This I know well because long since I knew
The song with which the South's gray nightingale
Salutes the dawn when gleaming stars grow pale,
As day's first light glows stronger and the hue
Of morn on rose-bright skies calls forth anew
The choral song of life on hill and dale !

Who knows the art by which the mocking bird
Pours all her subtle soul upon the night,
In tune with Jasmine odors and the light
Of the still moon ?   Surely her breast is stirred
By memories of spirit choir-chants heard
In skies where every melody is sung aright !

SYRINX.

M USIC is memory of a deathless past
        In those high spheres where every soul is fair !
Who knows and loves not song, let him beware
Lest he should wholly die and be outcast
Into some joyless place, dim, vague and vast,
With those who have no part, nor lot nor share
In heaven's clear harp-tones.   For they clasp but air,
Thinking to grasp their dearest hope at last !

So Pan for his lost hope was fain to die,
Gaining for Syrinx naught but her last sigh—
That low sweet tune slow-breathing South winds sing
Where tropic marsh-grass and white lilies spring
Among lone reeds and bright flamingoes wing
Their scarlet course against the deep blue sky !

DAPHNE.

M OST fair was Daphne! Ever fair to view
Is virgin Fame to him whose heart of fire
Flames forth in music from Apollo's lyre
Whose strings of flashing gold shall thrill anew
When tuned aright, as they were wont to do
Of old, when with the singer's high desire,
The burning god of light drew nigh and nigher
To her who spurned but that he might pursue!

Most fair is Daphne still, and still she turns
To a cold wreath of laurel for the brow
Of him whose youthful hope most hotly burns
When most she mocks him! For if I or thou
With fleet foot follow as she laughs and spurns,
So as of old, she still will cheat us now!

CASSANDRA.

THE fields are sweet with breath of May ; the skies
    Flecked with the dawn's pale gold, blush through their blue,
As though Morn told a tale of love to woo
The Day, a maiden coy who turns her eyes
Of azure downward, half afraid, and sighs
Lest her pure joy be known !   Shall not we too
Have morning faith to know that heaven is true,
And that sure faith alone can make us wise !

What though the night will come !   It is yet morn
And the day's light sufficeth for the day !
Turn from Cassandra !   Trust her lord, the sun,
Who all her vain foreboding puts to scorn
And from his face of glory rends away
The veil of mist by night's dim shadows spun !

THE DAUGHTER OF HERODIAS.

THE smitten cymbals with their tinkling rhyme,
    Chimed with the music of her glancing feet ;
Whirling and swirling, fleeter and more fleet,
Her white limbs flashed in rhythmic, pulsing time,
As she the daughter of that sun-bright clime,
With her fair body, bared their gaze to meet,
Danced for the Baptist's head before the seat
Where Herod sat enthroned.   So through all time,
Shall wanton beauty dance the truth to death ;
So through all years, shall they who truth deride,
Cry out at last in vain as Herod cried,
Consumed in his own flame, scorched by the breath
Of fiery lusts whereat hell shuddereth,
Hearing them shriek by whom truth was defied !

THE LADY OF THE LAKE.

THIS is for praise of that blest nameless fay
       Who gives to stricken weakness its due meed ;
Who comes to rescue at their utmost need
All those who faint and fail and yield the day !
Hers is the future.   Heed what she doth say :
" There is no failure.   Every noble deed
Shall wax from flower to fruit and bear the seed
Of a fair life that ne'er shall pass away ! "

In that calm land beneath the still lake's breast,
She waits for all who strive with sword or song
To free earth's weaklings from enthralling wrong.
With beckoning hand, she calls them to her rest,
In blest assurance that what each wrought best
Shall live and thrive and wax forever strong !

BATHSHEBA.

BEWARE always of what your heart desires,
Or you will gain it ! Even for them who stand,
The noblest of the earth, a fair-souled band,
Before heaven's parted gates and hear its choirs
Of white-robed seraphs with their golden lyres,
A path leads downward to a desolate land
Where pale souls wander through vast wastes of sand,
With hearts consumed by their own hidden fires !

Alas for Bathsheba, whose beauty drew
From heaven a singer's soul and brought it low !
Her body's bloom was fair as flowers that grow
By mountain lakes when spring makes all things new !
Alas for beauty's dower, and all who dare pursue
Their heart's desire until it brings them woe !

PENTHESILEA.

H EAVEN'S highest strength lies in the law of grace !
    She may be brave who cuts away the breast
To draw the bow, but love and truth are best,
And naught is stronger than the smiling face
Of beauty when pursuing blushes chase
Joy from low-lying coverts till they rest
On rose-red cheeks, all trembling from their quest,
But with their quarry caught and victors in the race !

Though force gives law to earth ; though blood be spilt ;
Though love with shackled hands must kneel to fear,
Yet steel is weaker still than pity's tear,
Shed for the sake of shamed and suffering guilt ;
For still shall grace prevail and love endear
Though sword-blades break and hands fail from the hilt !

CLYTIE.

THROUGH all the skies by mortal eyes unseen,
　　Fair shapes of light throng always, night and day !
Upward and downward on their shining way,
The vast, winged hosts of beauty, pure, serene,
Pass and repass, the earth and sky between !
Giving June dawns their charm of azure gray ;
Filling the spring with rare, faint scents of May ;
Blending on autumn hills their gold and green !

The sky's best gift of grace is light—more light !
Can you not guess why Clytie prays for sight,
Turning her face forever towards the sun ?
Who can express what wonders should be done,
Could we but see and know and feel aright
The glories we shall know when light is won ?

THE SPHINX.

A MONG dread silences she broods alone !
       Dead years of change and fate are heaped as sand
About her feet.   At her unvoiced command,
The mysteries sublime around Life's throne
Call out to centuries that wait unknown
About her gates.   (As is most meet, they stand
In endless, serried ranks on either hand
And gaze always into her face of stone !)

" What of the night ? "   Time's hoary warders call ;
" Is it far spent ?   Shall there be dawn and light ? "
And cloaked in cloud, the starry watchers all
Who keep their vigil round Life's fortress wall,
Cry out aloud from heaven with voice of might :
" Rejoice !   The darkness passes !   There is light ! "

THE HESPERIDES.

R EJOICE ! For night and fear are almost past ;
The glow of dawn shines on the tallest trees
In yon blest land of the Hesperides:
Rejoice ! There shall be light—clear light at last !
The glad day is at hand and many a mast,
When night is gone, shall dare the unknown seas
To seek the fruit that gives new life, and frees
Men's souls from night's dread ghosts and phantoms vast !

Rejoice ! The anchor-ropes are drawn by hands
That will not fail for labor of the oar,
Nor will their faces pale when Hope commands
And steers through perilous ways, untrod and hoar,
Of stormy seas between these forlorn lands
And the blest future's golden, shining shore !

MARY OF THE NATIVITY.

IF you can learn the secret of that day
  And be in soul and heart a little child,
All things are open to you ! Unbeguiled
By falsehood, hoar as Time and error gray
As the gray world itself, you shall have sway
O'er heavenly things, and spirits, undefiled
Of earth, on whom God's self has smiled,
Shall teach you all the secrets of heaven's way !

Lo, as that morning broke, the seraphim,
Souls that are mighty in the things they know,
Joined hands and sang a carol, soft and low
As the soft starlight that with morn grew dim !
Then as the sun rose, while they vanished slow,
They praised the Child and gave their thanks to Him !

MAID MARIAN.

A PRISONER, dying in a cheerless cell,
   Dreamed of Maid Marian and Sheerwood green !
He heard her sing: "When shaws bin sheen,
When hawthorns bloom in spring, 'tis well, 'tis well
To stray abroad with me and hear birds tell
Their mates so dear at morn what love doth mean ;
They sing full well what true, true love doth mean
When hawthorns bloom in spring by stream and fell !"

So sweet she sang the tall oaks bent to hear !
So soft and low she sang of love and spring,
The daffodils rejoiced to hear her sing ;
So clear she sang, the woodlands, far and near,
Waxed glad and rang as dream-born echoes ring,
Till that sad cell was filled with light and cheer !

ROSAMOND.

FAIR Rosamond was once the world's fair rose !
    Where is her beauty now when worms have fed
On cheeks whose sunny hues of damask red
Tempted a king's false kiss ?   No fair thing grows
In wood or field but it shall fail when snows
Are woven a shroud to cover Summer dead !
Alas, for springtime beauty that has fled
To some pale, empty world no mortal knows !

Yet this I know full well though roses fail,
Truth's spirit shall not fade for changing years ;
Brief beauty passes and we give it tears ;
False love endures no more when youth's cheeks pale,
But beauty's soul of truth shall still prevail
Beyond all time, throughout all skies and spheres !

PSYCHE IN HADES.

I SAW the small, unsightly, unborn soul
  Of a bright butterfly crawl here and there
On a broad leaf, in fretful, blind despair
Because it could not reach the higher goal
For which it strove, nor pass the leaf's control.
Alas, such grief has Psyche ere she rises fair
And floats in beauty through the summer air,
In tune with roundelays blithe field-larks trell,
Filling the still, blue skies with choral praise!
Alas, for Psyche's grief—for the blind night
Of Hades and its paths devoid of light!
Alas, that she must wander through dim ways
Of the gray underworld ere she can raise
Bright wings that bear her on her skyward flight!

MAB ASLEEP.

I SAW Queen Mab asleep beneath the shade
   Of a blue violet's longest, greenest leaf,
Where by all human eyes she lay unseen
Save mine.   Far off the strong-armed reapers sang
Their harvest song.   Grave kine and mild-eyed sheep
Drank from the stream among the rushes green
Where water lilies lean their stately heads,
Sleeping because their fairies are asleep.

Beneath the rowan shade where violets grow,
She lay asleep.   Her face was like the leaf
Of a white rose, unclosing in the light
Of early dawn and full of the rare grace
Of springtime mornings in that kingdom fair
Where bright-winged Mab rules all the fairy race!

MARY AND THE MAGI.

L OVE is most wise and potent though it lies
    A child new-born, upon its mother's breast.
Above all stars shone its fair star that morn,
When with the censer's smoke, rare odors rose,
As bending low, the mighty seers who know
All deep truths of the dawn-stars and the skies,
Gave him their worship though forlorn he lay,
Heaven's Truth new-born among the kine that day !

Still shines the star of faith in skies afar,
And whoso will may follow as of old
To where truth lies, all-wise on Mary's breast.
Fair shines the star, but bleak and hot and bare,
Are the vast sands between love's lands and these
Wherefrom the Magian starts upon his quest.

ROSEMARY.

L ITTLE know they who think Rosemary dead,
    For she is dancing in bright fairy rings
In fair Glenavon where the crocus springs—
The yellow crocus with the white one wed—
Among the snows ere winter days are sped !
The daoine-shee loved her as she loved fair things,
And when she floats with them on radiant wings,
Though we have lost her, let no tear be shed !

She loved white hollyhocks that blossomed tall
Behind red roses by the garden wall !
She stretched her small hands to them on the day
The daoine-shee came to bear her soul away !
Knowing their speech, she smiled to hear them call,
Nor though she loved us, could she dare delay !

OUR LADY OF ANGELS.

THOUGH hate may scoff, there is a great, white throne,
    A heaven of light and glory where the sound
Of universal harmonies profound,
Thrills rescued souls as with an echoed tone
Blent from blest deeds and all the high thoughts known
In their own lives. And there, with glories crowned,
Where Mary stands, the ransomed hosts around
Cry " Hail !" to her whose grace is made their own !

She stands amid a mighty multitude,
The unnumbered souls for whom her Son was slain,
They come from nameless graves in many lands,
With robes of white and radiant wings bright-hued,
To give her praise and thanks for all her pain,
Holding fair palms of victory in their hands !

THE NEREID.

WITH a girl's gold hair the Nereid strings
       The harp she made from a lover's breast-bone !
Strange, holy and rare is that lyre's clear tone ;
Strange, magical, fair are the songs she sings.
Wild, thrilling and high her melody rings
As in depths profound, she sits all alone,
Under the sea on an opaline throne,
Crowned with glittering gems the sea-snake brings
From argosies wrecked for her sweet song's sake.
"Come down, you weary ones, deep down to me ;"
"Come down," she entreats you ; "Why, why will you break
Your hearts for a dream of dim mystery?
Come hither, deep down, and my songs shall make
Your sad souls gladsome and fearless and free ! "

ILSE.

A T the hidden door in the Ilsenstein
     The Prince smote boldly and cried out her name !
Three times he had smitten ere bright Ilse came
To give him pebbles and cones of the pine.
" My gifts " said Ilse, "shall make you divine ;
For all these are honors and this is fame ;
And this I call praise and a lordly name
And these are jewels that sparkle and shine ! "

Not once, not twice but three times must they smite
On the Ilsenstein with a mail-clad hand
Ere fair Ilse will come at their command,
To bring them her jewels and honors bright
That shine with a wonderful, elfin light
To dazzle men's eyes in every land !

BRUNHILD.

IN the North stands a castle girt with fire
And in it a sleeping Valkyrie lies
With Odin's thorn-spell on her fast-closed eyes!
To him who has conquered the dragon dire
And broken her slumber's magical gyre,
She will teach three runes to make him wise
As a man may be on earth ere he dies ;
For she is fair Brunhild, your heart's desire!

Fair are the charmed banners on Brunhild's wall ;
All golden they glow in the morn's first beams
In that olden, magical land of dreams
Where gleams through the mist her turrets so tall ;
And fair the bright vision of beauty seems
When Brunhild arises at Sigurd's call !

QUEEN HOLDA.

A Choral Ode.

ALONE, unknown, she stands beside the sea
　　Where round the dark rune-stone the gray gulls cry ;
Where round that magic stone the sad waves sigh !
The song she sings is charmed !　Wild, wild and free,
It rings with wondrous sound of melody ;
It rings the world around till earth and sky
Thrill with its magic tune ; and far and nigh,
The air is sweet with flowers that soon shall be !

Bright Holda comes with voice of golden song ;
Rare days of light and joy her spell shall bring ;
She will repay with gladness of the spring
And fragrant breath of May the winter's wrong.
Rejoice, sad heart ! the glad air is athrong
With flower-crowned fays who dance to hear her sing !

CHARLOTTE CORDAY.

W ITH steadfast eye she watched the quivering light
         Flash from the bright blade of the guillotine;
Nor shrank from death nor from the dread, unseen,
Stern terrors of the day beyond Death's night,
Where waited her the Judge within whose sight
Her hand relentless, drove the dagger keen
To the foul heart of that base wretch and mean
Whose lust had been her suffering country's blight!

Though girt in mail of power and fenced in pride,
He needs beware whom woman counts heaven's foe.
Be it soon or late, his soul shall surely know
What justice means.   For when heaven is defied,
If no strong champion comes to take God's side,
Her own weak hand shall strike fate's deadliest blow!

MADAM ROLAND.

THOUGH in thy hallowed name, O Liberty,
　　Were marshalled once the rebel hosts of hell,
Still shall the tongues of freemen learn to tell
Thy praise from hearts that burn with love of thee!
Above earth's lordliest names thy name shall be.
Sister and nurse of Peace, does he not well,
Who strikes a blow for thee and dares to tell
The truth of heaven that makes men brave and free?

Though they who love thee die as Roland died,
By tyrant, mob or law condemned to shame,
Thou art most fair, O Freedom! and thy name
Shall wax in greatness while the stars abide
And in the skies God's glorious will proclaim:—
That truth shall make men free whate'er betide !

THE CAULDRON OF CARIDWAIN.

THROUGH spring and summer, a year and a day,
   Must boil the charmed cauldron of Caridwain
Ere Guion, the dwarf, can be born again
As the bard of the everlasting lay,
Whose soul endures from forever to aye ;
Who stood by the cross when the Christ was slain ;
Who wrought with the builders on Shinar's plain ;
Whose abode was the dawn-star's primal ray !

When the three charmed drops fell on Guion's tongue,
Sweet, marvellous sweet, were the songs he sung ;
The wind's wild swiftness, his spirit outran
And blent with the heavenly spirit of man ;
To the thought eternal his freed thought sprung
And he lived all life in his one life's span !

THE CURSE OF CARIDWAIN.

A THRICE-BORN soul has Talyesin, the bard,
  For Caridwain has made his thoughts divine ;
Upon his radiant brow, blest memories shine
Of far-off skies, dim, blue and many-starred ;
Yet this shall ever be his life's reward,
To taste salt tears until he loves their brine,
To give fair pearls and bear the scorn of swine
Until his heart is but a broken shard !

By night and by day through all the long year,
Must boil the charmed cauldron of Caridwain
To make the three drops to her magic dear ;
And never, ah never, never again
Shall he who tastes live a man among men
And be glad in his soul with his fellows here !

URD.

WHEN Bragi came where Urd's clear fountain flows
      Beneath the roots of mighty Iggdrasill,
He felt the universal pulses thrill
With the same thought that shapes a summer rose,
As it has made creative light that flows
From stars and suns to blend its strength until
Earth's smallest flower shows the same might and skill
The vast, blue dome of star-lit midnight shows!

As Bragi came, the gray, eternal Urd,
She who hath been forever, who shall be
When there is neither earth, nor sky nor sea,
Rose from her seat and spoke the fatal word
That makes the skald and sets his chained soul free ;
And Asgard sang for joy as Bragi heard!

THE GARDEN OF IDUNA.

IDUNA'S garden lies where blue skies smile
  Above a vale where the shy brown-thrush calls
His mate when, hushed and still, calm evening falls.
The glowing sun sinks low, and pile on pile
From golden clouds, the gnomes with elfin guile,
Build Asgard's shining towers and flaming walls,
Where with great Odin in celestial halls,
Blest heroes quaff their foaming mead, the while
Bright Bragi gives them praise for glorious deeds.
Great Odin listens and fair Baldur heeds
The harp's high strains as Bragi gives them praise
For all their hero-pains in earthly days ;
But my weak soul, the sweet Iduna leads
Along her fragrant paths and flower-grown ways !

IDUNA AND THE RUNES OF BRAGI.

B LEST is the soul blue-eyed Iduna leads
     With soft control, along her lofty ways,
In peaceful skies where after weary days,
All troubles cease; where no heart bleeds ;
Where faith and hope lean not on broken reeds ;
Where, brighter for earth's doubting and delays,
Calm truth shines out at last in hallowed rays
Of fairest light whereby the wanderer reads
From Bragi's scroll all he had sought to know.
High are the runes of Bragi and most wise
Is the charmed song Iduna sings, when low
The sun sinks in the west, and all the skies
Shine with the beams on Valhall's towers that glow,
When Asgard gleams too bright for mortal eyes !

THE FLOWERS OF IDUNA.

B RIGHT shines the sunset on high Asgard's towers
    And fair is Valhall with its myriad rooms ;
But brighter and more fair that garden blooms
Where through eternal summer's odorous hours
Iduna tends with magic art her flowers—
The strange, unearthly blossoms whose perfumes
The light-alfs gather when the moon illumes
That high, enchanted plaisance where all powers,
All thoughts, all wishes of earth's purest minds
Find a new birth in color and rare scent
Of the strange blossoms sweet Iduna tends !
Most blest is he who meets her there and finds
With her charmed flowers, his life-thought fully blent
In that fair garth where summer never dies !

THE APPLES OF IDUNA.

IDUNA'S fruit is sweet and good to see ;
   She has three gold-hued apples which once grew
In her fair garden where all love is true ;
Where every heart is pure and all souls free
From thoughts which if they came to you and me
Would bring us shame and bitterness and rue !
Ah, may no thought of shame e'er come to you
And may you pluck fair fruit from Idun's tree !

The mighty gods must come, by night and day,
To eat Iduna's fruit of ruddy gold ;
For if they came not, they would fade away,
Growing all sere, and worn and grim and old,
Wan as wan death, gray as hoar Time is gray
And cold at heart as sated Sin is cold !

IDUNA AND HELA.

STRAYING at night beyond her garden's bound,
  Iduna met sad Hela, face to face.
" Lo, I am death !" said Hela, "and this grace
I crave of thee who art life's great queen, crowned
To reign where joys of light do most abound :—
Grant that all souls who lie in that drear place
Of Nostrand, may look on thy radiant face
And from thy lips learn the three runes profound
Which wake the dead from love of their foul sin !"
With pallid brow and lips whereon no red
Blent with that ashen hue we dread to see
On cheeks we love, did Hela thus begin
Pleading for them, the long-forgotten dead,
Who chose in life, each what his death should be !

IDUNA IN THE IRONWOOD.

I DUNA wandered in the ironwood
   Far to the East of Midgard where sits Shame ;
Ancient and gray, she feeds a cauldron's flame.
Wherein fell deeds of all base womanhood
Bubbled and seethed as there the goddess stood.
'' Who art thou ?" said Iduna.   '' Is thy name
Not Death in Life, and art thou not the same
Foul Sin who bore the hateful Fenris brood ?''

Shame grinned and stirred her cauldron round and round,
But answered not !   Then as Iduna turned
To leave in haste that grim and dreadful spot,
The foul hag laughed aloud, and at the sound,
The cauldron's flame burned blue and hissing hot
And Outgard shuddered to its utmost bound !

IDUNA AND OUTGARD.

LEANING from Asgard's lofty wall, she saw,
    Far down below, through depths of cold, blue space,
Dead worlds of shame and radiant worlds of grace,
Swinging in tune to a harmonious law,—
A rune of power, most holy, without flaw,
The heavenly song that in the highest place,
Veiled spirits sing before the flaming face
Of Him whose lightest thought has might to draw
Asgard's high towers to ruin and nothingness.
Far down in space she saw this little earth,
With its blind pain and shame, its death and birth ;
Its joy, its mirth, its wrongs and sore distress !
" All humankind, " she said, " shall Bragi bless,
And with high songs raise men to nobler worth ! "

IDUNA IN VALHALL.

VALHALL'S high Hall of Spears shone all aglow
   With ruddy light and loudly Asgard rang
With clamor of proud wassail and wild clang
Of blood-stained swords which once wrought bale and woe
To make the fame of heroes who, a-row,
Feast now where round the walls their banners hang !
So once they sat a-row while hoar skalds sang
Their deeds at Yule-tide feasts on earth below !

" Skoal ! " cried Jarl Eric, as the mead he poured
Into a bowl wrought from grim Hakon's skull ;
"Skoal, and drink hale to Hela, sad and pale !
To bright Iduna, too, skoal and drink hale !
Skoal, three times skoal, and let each bowl be full
When sweet Iduna feasts at Odin's board ! "

IDUNA AND THE HARP OF BRAGI.

B RIGHT Bragi thrust aside his harp of gold,
 Wrenching away each living, flaming string;
" Ah, woe is me !" he cried.   " I cannot sing;
My soul is sad ; my heart grows sere and old ;
My voice is cracked and thin ; my songs are cold ;
They ring no more as they were wont to ring,
Nor have they strength to soar on mounting wing
As once they soared when they were true and bold !
Ah, sweet Iduna, canst thou give the fire
To quicken to new life and strength again
A weary spirit and an outworn lyre?
That I may sing once more the clear, high strain
Which soothes all woe, makes lighter every pain
And bids each wretched human heart aspire?"

IDUNA AND SURT.

" I COME " Iduna said " to seek the fire
 Of Muspelheim wherein the Spirit dwells,
Who rules all worlds, all heavens and all hells !
Asgard is sad, for tuneless is the lyre
Whereto bright Bragi sang each pure desire,
Each high and holy rune just Friga tells
And every thought in Odin's mind that dwells
To bless mankind and raise their weak souls higher ! "

" Alas ! " Surt said ; " that fire thou ne'er canst see !
If thou couldst know the secret of this land,
Even though a goddess, thou shouldst surely die !
Not Odin's self knows that high mystery ;
Vainly with idle prayers thou troublest me ;
Back, back ! " he cried, and shook his flaming brand !

IDUNA AND BALDUR.

FROM his high throne in Hela's shadowy land,
   Dead Baldur rose and kissed Iduna's cheek.
Sad ghosts had joy in death to hear him speak,
Who by the gentle breath of his command,
Wrought flowers and beauty in each barren land,
And brought to earth, once dreary, cold and bleak,
Bright summer hours, when love, no longer weak,
Has might to conquer all the Jotun band !

" Fear not !" said Baldur ; " Bragi's loss is gain ;
He shall be strongest of all gods above.
Never in vain sings he to human ears
Who learns from his own grief to pity tears ;
Who learns to spare the weak from his own pain,
And strings anew his harp with chords of love !"

IDUNA AND LOKE.

CURST Loke came clothed in robes of shining white ;
    He is the vilest of the Nighthag's kin ;
But yet his face shone radiant as young Sin
When to fresh youth it offers fair delight.
As a winged prince of light-alves, pure and bright,
He came Iduna's fruit of life to win,
That through her shame the sooner might begin
Dread ragnarok with all its ruin and blight !

Iduna knows a rune of three-fold grace
With which she guards the treasure Loke would take ;
And when she spoke it for her pure love's sake,
The fell sprite shrieked and vanished.   In the place
Where he had kneeled to work her soul's disgrace,
Hardby her feet writhed a foul, hissing snake !

THE BANSHEE.

I HEARD the banshee call ! Her voice is mild
   As the low wash of waves on sunlit strands,
Where blue seas break in music on white sands
In lands where pain by sweet dreams is beguiled.
As in my arms at dawn, I held a child,
I heard the banshee's call.   And still she stands
There in my hall at dawn as when its hands
(Its sweet, small hands) the child stretched out and smiled.

Albeit her face is wan, it has the grace
Of moonlight falling pale on rapid streams
And scintillating through their jewelled spray.
So ever seems to me the banshee's face,
As in my hall she stands at dawn of day,
Calling me to wake from sleep and troubled dreams !

EVE IN EXILE.

B RAVE in distress and greater than the stain
    Of serpent sin upon her womanhood,
Before lost Eden's gate our Mother stood
And gazed into the future where all pain
Of hers and all her sons shall be their gain.
For spite of fate and all the adder brood
Of night and terror, he who bears his rood,
Shall win his heaven, nor shall the mark of Cain
Doom him to that black pit where serpents hiss
The primal curse !   No soul that strives shall fail
Nor be betrayed to death by Judas kiss.
Against the grave all souls of truth prevail
And win to heavenly bliss through Calvary's bale.
Know this !   There is no greater law than this !

THE PERI.

THE Peri floated, a white cloud on high,
 O'er the crowded town at the close of day.
Far down on the plain where great Bagdad lay,
She gazed with a tear in her pitying eye ;
Then straight she turned, by the spell of a sigh,
To a gleaming mote in the sun's last ray,
And fell in the room where a sick child lay,
To give it a dream of the clear, blue sky !

When the Peri floats at the noontide hour
Where Bagdad town spreads vast on the plain;
She sees from on high the woe and the pain
Of its weak souls, crushed by the pride and power
Of those who have robbed them of freedom's dower,
And she cries : " Alas ! are these lives in vain ? "

MODGUDA.

WHEN I rode to the Yellow bridge that lies
    Between Midgard and Helheim, vast and cold,
Modguda stayed me.   Yet I could behold
Strange, ghostly sights that no man ere he dies,
Beholds, except he see with Odin's eyes
Or the skald's vision !   On that bridge of gold,
I saw a mighty host, the young, the old,
The fair-haired and the gray, the fools, the wise,
The humble and the great of this strange earth !
A mighty spectre band, by night and day
They crowd the entrance to the narrow way
That leads men to the land of death in birth.
But when I gazed, I thought on days of mirth
In shining Gladheim and I could not stay !

MARY AND THE CHILD.

FROM what mysterious, unseen, distant skies,
   Far, far beyond star-gazing Magi's ken,
Came this child-soul to know the ways of men
And bear their pains? Lo, as new-born he lies,
Eternity looks out through his clear-seeing eyes,
Fixed on his mother's fair, pale face, as when
Ten thousand blessed spirits cried, Amen !
Hearing his will to live in human guise.

This day, I saw a child lie as he lay.
Tender and sweet it was and newly-born ;
Unmeet for life's rough way seemed its small feet,
And its fair brow unmeet to wear the thorn
That truth wears now as on the primal day
When Christ stood calm at haughty Herod's seat !

AILEEN AROON.

A Song.

A H, how could you leave me, Aileen Aroon,
    Who gladly would die for your sweet love's sake?
Your beauty is bright as light on the lake
When, rising at midnight, the full-orbed moon—
(The deep-bosomed maid whose rays are in tune
To the white, silent music shining stars make!)
When the radiant moon through gray clouds doth break
To gaze on your bright face, Aileen Aroon!

Come back, come back to your Carrol, Aileen!
Smile now as you smiled in glad days of yore
In our play-time of life when Maytime was green
And fragrant with flowers that bloomed round your door!
Lean on this fond heart as once you would lean,
Aileen mavourneen, and leave me no more!

SWANHILD, THE VALKYRIE.

A T sunset, under dark and clouded skies,
  Unknown among the dead, Jarl Hakon lay.
As one who breathes his life and hope away
And curses Odin as he fails and dies,
He lay alone, the death mist on his eyes.
Then from high Asgard's bright, unending day,
Swift as an arrow or the dawn-star's ray,
Came Swanhild, bravest, truest and most wise
Of battle-maids who are the hopes of men !
And bending by his side in that dark fen,
That bloody marsh of death, she cleared the mist
Of Helheim from his eyes so that he wist
All Valhall's glories with his dying ken
As his pale cheek the gracious Swanhild kissed.

RANHILD.

THE breakers roar hoarse as the rising gale
 Fans fiercely the funeral pyre's red flame,
Where Thorgrim lies in the arms of his dame !
Dead lies the dread Jarl, but living and pale
Sits his bride where the black ship's crackling sail
Above her bent head, burns red as the name
The Vikings left in the lands where they came
With woe and slaughter, with ravin and bale !

Pale Ranhild sits steadfast with tearless eye
As the storm drives the flaming ship to sea !
She hears the wild breakers roar loud on the lea ;
She feels the fierce heat as the flames mount high,
But holding her dead lord's head on her knee, ·
She shows how a Berserker's wife can die !

THE MAID OF THE VAN.

A Ballad.

UNTENDED the sheep are pent in their fold ;
    Unfed are the kine, unreaped the ripe corn !
To the lake in the mountains Llewellen has gone
Where the Maid of the Van with her girdle of gold,
Rows her glittering boat when o'er mountain and wold,
O'er lake and o'er fountain, the wonderful horn
Of the shy queen of Elfland gives warning of dawn
And the bright stars of morning grow pallid and cold !

Though stars fade away, soon again they shall burn,
But never again shall Llewellen return !
He has gone to the mountain far, dim and remote,
Where the maid of the Van rows her crystalline boat ;
Where in the charmed air elfin melodies float
That none save her poets and lovers shall learn !

THE KORRIGAN.

A Ballad.

L OUD wails his young bride for handsome Lord Nain ;
　Cold, cold is the bride-bed in which he must sleep ;
In the clay of the churchyard, narrow and deep,
They have made him a chamber where sunshine and rain
Shall fall on the roof all unheeded and vain ;
Ne'er again shall he waken to laugh or to weep ;
To ride in wild foray or love-tryst to keep,
For the spell of the korr-maid has wrought him his bane !

She sat by the fountain and combed her bright hair ;
Red gold was her comb, and the witch-spell she said
Was as sweet as the tune of the melodies rare
The moon-fairies sing in the uppermost air !
Ah, weep for the young bride whose brief joy has fled !
Ah, weep for Lord Nain in his deep narrow bed !

UNDINE.

UNDINE was but a rainbow, seen at eve
    Above the sea, mixed with the crystal dew
That shines upon the violet's petals blue.
From such brief, dream-wrought lives, the sunbeams weave
Enchanted shapes most potent to deceive
The haunted thoughts of poets.   Yet she grew
Through pain of love immortal, wise and true,
Gaining a soul the while she learned to grieve !

Fair lives of joy shall pass and fade away ;
They last but as sea-mist and blown, white foam ;
But twice-born souls of truth shall live for aye
And in far heavens find an eternal home,
A fairer life, a rarer, purer day,
Enduring as the sky's blue, star-set dome !

THE MAID OF ELLE.

WE are but dreamers in a blind, gray night
　　　Where here and there a star gleams clear and shows
The way to that fair land he finds who knows
What children know, who through pure faith have sight
For unseen worlds where, by love's grace and might,
They who seek light will know what heaven still shows
When faith glows bright as Northern midnight glows
Where polar skies stream with auroral light.

In that blest land, the best and bravest dwell!
There flows Urd's fount, and there the Maid of Elle
Will kiss your cheek and lead you by the hand
To glowing springs of light where the bright band
Of souls who seek for truth shall understand
The lore wise Odin learned at Mimir's well!

THEKLA AT ANTIOCH.

A LL round the circus ran a low, soft sound
Of women's voices ! Many a fair, proud face
Shone bright as dames of high, heroic race
Stretched out turned thumbs the vast arena round,
Giving the death sign.   By their slaves unbound,
The tigress slowly entered that dread place
And fixed her glowing eyes on Thekla's face.
Firm stood the virgin, waiting to be crowned,
As they are crowned who for truth's sake, bear shame
And dare to die, outcast, despised, alone !
The maiden stood with her pure body bared
By shameless hands ! Creeping, the tigress came
Nearer and yet more near ! Her fierce eyes glared,
But Thekla stood and prayed before God's throne !

THE PERI BEFORE EBLIS.

W HERE Eblis sat upon his golden throne,
   A fair, pure Peri stood with fearless mien ;
Her form was heavenly light.   Her soul serene
Was harmony divine, the sweet, clear tone
Harp-players make who tune their harps alone,
Far in deep woods when spring grows glad and green.
The Peri's soul is peace.   But I have seen
The heart of Eblis.   'Tis a red-hot stone.

Around his throne, earth's lords and masters stand
And in each breast glows a slow-burning flame
That through eternal ages shall not cease !
With one accordant voice, that haughty band
Hail him their chief and laud his dreadful name.
But Eblis scorns them since praise gives not peace !

PEGGY.

FLOWERS have a heavenly meaning and a spell
     Of infinite, eternal tenderness ;
In pity for blind, burning selfishness,
For pain of hearts on fire with passions fell,
God's kindness clothes with flowers the plains of hell.
High angels soothe with flowers our worst distress
As I most surely know.   Yet none less,
Hood's Peggy scorns a rose and hates its smell.

And I know why ; for lately I have seen
Her wandering sick and ragged through the streets,   .
Hawking the roses out sweet Margaret wears.
Ah, blest is he who pities and who spares !
Who learns that love is best and kindness meet !
For he shall find what flowers and mercy mean.

XANTIPPE.

X ANTIPPE has been needlessly maligned
     By all historians of ancient date
Because upon her husband's broad, bald pate
She once threw slop !   But no impartial mind
A cause for blame in that just act can find ;
For these same great philosophers exasperate
The saints themselves, gadding abroad to prate,
Leaving their patient wives to stop behind.

And then the impartial judgment sees,
When from above her pail of slops she throws,
Naught but her true desire to educate
The philosophic mind into a higher state.
Men are what women make them, and that shows
Xantippe's scolding made great Socrates !

TO JENNY.

" Cum tu Lydia Telephi—"

JENNY, 'tis now just fifteen years ago
   Since you discarded me for Howard Pell.
Have you forgotten—I remember well—
The blackness of my deep and utter woe?
How hard and vainly I strove not to show
My burning hate for him when you would tell
That in the last mazourka he danced well
And that his black moustache became him so !

I'm still a bachelor and somewhat blue
While you have six small children and the gout ;
But I am told your Howard's good to you,
And he's a first-rate fellow I've no doubt !
Ah, happy they who from the courts keep out,
Bound by a love that is forever true !

TO MISS BETTY STARLING.

" Est mihi nonum—"

M Y dear Miss Betty :—Come on Wednesday night,
   And be sure not to fail.   We've baked a cake
And in their beds are growing for your sake
Roses both pink and red.   They will look bright,
If you will place them in the laces white
About your throat.   I think Jack's heart will break,
If you are late, or worse, if you should take
A naughty notion this small note to slight.

Be good to Jack ; for that young Woodhouse Strong
Is a sad rake not fit to tie your shoe.
'Twill be Jack's birthday.   He's half-dead for you.
Now don't forget.   Please come ; and if you do,
Be sure and bring your new guitar along
And sing for us.   For care is soothed by song !

TO CHLOE.

M Y fawn-like Chloe, you do well to shun
      That rascal, Flaccus, who's a devotee
Of Venus and of Bacchus too. For he
Would surely break your heart and think it fun ;
With you he'd do as he's already done
With Phyllis, Glycera and Lalage ;
With Nerea, Chloris and Phidyle ;
And after them with many another one.

Believe me, Chloe, you have cause to fear,
As very well your anxious mother knows
Whene'er she finds a smooth-tongued rascal near.
He'd pull you as a small boy pulls a rose.
Unless you use your thorns, you're gone, my dear,
For when you're pulled, he'll never heed your woes !

LUCY NOË.

SWEET Lucy Noë, learn to trust the sky !
    Nor seek from gypsies what your fate must be ;
Nor shuffle false, deceitful packs to see
From jacks for low and puff-cheeked kings for high
What next year brings !   Whether we live or die,
Let us two sit unvext to-day and free
From fear and care !   If you but dare trust me,
You'll smile, my dear !   'Tis better than to sigh !

We shall do well enough !   Nay, never fear !
Seize on the day and live your very best !
Heaven knows the future ; while our skies are clear,
We'll hope our hopes and leave to heaven the rest !
So now, sweet Lucy, stand close by me here
And let me pin this red rose on your breast !

SALLY.

" Quis Multa Gracilis."

WHO'S dallying with fair Sally's cruel snare?
    What perfumed youth woos her with many a vow
There in the blooming, rose-grown arbor now?
For whom with care she parts her golden hair
In artful artlessness !   Let him beware
Whome'er she greets with gracious smile and bow,
For if her wiles to win him he'll allow,
She'll break his heart and bring him to despair !

Much will he suffer as I suffered once
Before I learned that smiling seas grow rough.
You please me, charming Sally, well enough ;
I still can love a flirt, but I'm no dunce,
And rascal Cupid's sharpest arrow blunts
Against my heart as I grow old and tough !

TO BELLA.

" Nox erat et caelo fulgehat luna sereno—"

'TWAS night !   In the clear sky the bright moon shone
And from on high the listening stars could hear !
You swore that I should be forever dear
And that you'd love me truly and alone
While glistening Dian keeps her crystal throne ;
While twinkling stars wink dim above and peer
Out from behind their clouds fleece-lined, in fear
Lest what they think of lover's vows be known.

O Bella, dear, I grieve to hear you say,
After all that, so frigidly that I
Am but a brother to you now.   To-day,
You walked with Dick and passed me coldly by ;
Though he struts now, I don't expect to die
Until this self-same trick on him you play !

LYDDY.

M Y dearest Lyddy, come sit by me here,
    For there is a secret I fain would know :—
Why does young Payne Farrington love you so
That tennis and football he doesn't go near?
The head of his cane he sucks till I fear
His brain will be turned ere his ideas flow
And he learns some sensible way to show
What he burns to tell you, Lyddy, my dear !

If he knew, my Lyddy, the end of that—
Had he nursed six children through colds and croup ;
With the whooping cough had he heard them whoop ;
Had he the knowledge that's under my hat,
Would he sit around and pule and droop,
And be such a miserable, love-sick flat ?

EDITH.

" Passer deliciae meae puellae—"

WOULD I could envy Edith's ugly pug,
    That curled-tail monster whose cold, clammy nose
The dear girl kisses while her plump cheek glows,
Redder than bright Jack roses ere the slug
Has touched 'em !   How her virgin charms would tug
At my old heart-strings if she did not pose,
Holding that pampered, round-paunched rascal, Bose,
In her fair arms to kiss his snub-nosed mug !

His well-soaped hide is wrinkled up with fat ;
He's haughty as a bloated millionaire,
Because he knows no human pup would dare
Attempt to put a paw where his are at.
Dear Edith trains him carefully for that ;
And if she'll wash her mouth, I'll kiss her there !

ON THE DEATH OF EDITH'S PUG.

" Lugete, O Veneres Cupidinesque—"

REJOICE, ye Cupids, Edith's pug is dead !
   Never again, shall her vermilion kiss
Waste on his nose what had been perfect bliss
If rightly placed.   But Edith's eyes are red ;
So let a billion salty tears be shed
In grief for Bose !   How sadly we shall miss
Those uppish airs he gave himself, I wiss,
Waddling, short-legged, behind her as she led
Him by a ribbon round his fat-creased neck !
But cease, dear Edith, cease at length to weep !
Life is too short to waste it in such sighs !
The tears you've shed would make at least a peck ;
So cheer up now and dry your swollen eyes
Though Bose is wrapped in an eternal sleep !

BONNYBELLE.

COME kiss me, my Bonnybelle, red-cheeked lass,
    For this day I am come to forty year !
You look as your mother once looked, my dear,
Some twenty years syne when I was an ass,
And Thackeray says—but we'll let that pass !
For though grizzling of hair the brain doth clear,
Mine's black must grow grizlier yet, my dear,
Ere I make light of the worth of a lass !

Your cheeks are red, but no redder I ween,
Nor your eyes more sparkling than hers were then
As a coy, smiling lass just turned seventeen ;
(And a sweeter yet I never have seen !)
Ah, a fig for wisdom and all wise men,
If heaven would but make me a boy again !

MARQUISE.

YOU scarcely have at six years old, Marquise,
　　The same fine, high-bred air you had at three.
You're losing tone in our society,
As I can not deny.　But tell me, please,
For what small sin they banished you to these
Low-lying lands upon Time's farthest lea
And on sin's windward side, where I can see
You're lowering to our level by degrees.

Alas, you did a human thing to-day,
An ill-bred thing your father might have done,
Who knows all naughtiness beneath the sun.
Come tell me, Marchioness, and then go play,
And if the star that lost you, has another ray
Clear as your soul, may it soon send us one !

MILDRED.

M ILDRED, the little short-tailed, wise, shy wren,
There on the rose-bush, has three eggs of blue,
One for each year the angels have brought you
Since that remembered April morning when
You shed your wings and came to live with men.
You did not look as if you ever flew,
But none the less your sage, old father knew
The whole deep truth about you even then !

Ten thousand years ago, you had a nest—
(Ten hundred thousand years are but a day
Up in far skies where small, bright angels play—)
Ten thousand years ago, you had a nest,
Where every day, a pale-blue egg you'd lay
Among pink rose-buds.   Pink buds you liked the best.

LITTLE BO PEEP.

O UR little Bo Peep ere she went away
    To seek her lost sheep in a fairer land,
Loved spring and rare sunshine and lilies grand—
The queenly lilies that reign for a day !
She loved the sweet singing of birds in May
When flowers are springing through all the land
And that is why in her tight-closed hand,
She held a white rose as asleep she lay !

Our little Bo Peep ere she went to sleep,
Had deep, smiling dimples and wide brown eyes ;
She knew it best to be merry and wise,
A waste of sweet spring-time to sigh and weep.
Now close at her head as alone she lies,
Is a white, stone lamb from her flock of sheep !

TO MY MOTHER.

MOTHER, time's snow has fallen upon your hair
    These many years since you with yearning gaze
Watched one well-loved go unreturning ways,
And gave him tears.   I know not if there are
Women of wit more burning, forms more fair,
For earth has not another one whose praise
Your son would sing throughout all years and days,
If idle rhymes could but repay your care !

Your prayer for me when Sabbath evening chimes
Sound sweet upon the air of placid Junes,
Has made my soul more meet for all fair tunes
Which fill with melody the unseen climes
Where deathless singers with their wondrous runes
Make music with a magic spell for after times.

IN MARY'S GARDEN.

IN Mary's garden, fair maids stand a-row
   Beside a violet bed fringed with heartsease !
You will not find six sweeter maids than these ;
(I ask your pardon !   What I say, I know !)
For not one is contrary and they grow
So good and kind that every one who sees
Has often said that they, by slow degrees,
Grow more like flowers.   And that, I think, is so !

Have you not seen these six fair maids of ours?
One is fourteen and growing very tall ;
One is just middle-size and one is small ;
And when they're good and kind, they seem like flowers.
Yes, in my mind, I deem these maids of ours
The sweetest, best and brightest of them all !

TO LOULA.

"BE good, sweet maid, and let who will be clever !"
    So a dear friend of ours advises you ;
But you may be both good and clever too !
Let that be always your assured endeavor ;
Learn from your garden's flowers and you will never
Forget what lilies teach when wet with dew :—
That purest souls are fairest and most true
And fragrant, unstained thoughts are wise forever !

The stars are high but let your thoughts reach higher
Until it finds the all-pervading mind,
And if your soul be dumb, in self confined,
Pray that the seraphim may touch with fire
Your lips, that you may voice each pure desire
And heaven's true thought in your own thoughts may find !

TO A SEMPSTRESS.

YOU who once read with me the Mantuan's page ;
  You who might boast the high Heraklid blood,
Have spent the best days of your womanhood,
The fairest years of all your youthful age
In toil so hard for such a scanty wage
That I can see your work stained as if blood
You gave in sacrifice to motherhood
And the pure love that doth your thoughts engage !

A noble woman is God's highest work,
And though your name of light I do not call,
I shut my love for it down deep within
A soul where still this pride and hope will lurk,
That you who are the truest of them all
May feel no shame to hear me claim you kin !

MOTHER GOOSE.

GREAT Mother Goose, who art the very chief
      Of sweet New England singers, hail, all hail !
The tooth of carking time shall not prevail
Against thee !   Though we lose belief
In bards more sage and learn with deepest grief
That they're no Homers, ne'er shall cease or fail
Thy praises ; ne'er thy burning glories pale !
Thou mighty mistress of the lyre, thou chief
Of Runic song, teach us thy magic art,
That we may surely reach the human heart
With deathless strains which still from age to age,
The pains of earth's long childhood shall assuage.
For they who scorn thy rhymes, in vain do wage
Their puny war against Time's conquering dart !

THE WOMAN IN THE BASKET.

O SEE the wise woman, how high she flies,
   Ninety and nine times as high as the moon !
Will she descend and end her work full soon?
Or will she stay till from the upper skies,
Those cobwebs gray which baffle prying eyes,
She clears away?   Will she bring down the tune
The spheres sing?   Will she learn the rune
The man in the full moon tells to the wise?

Up in her basket this good woman went
To straighten out the great bear's crooked tail !
She'll not descend until her breath is spent !
So do not ask it !   But she's growing pale ;
And if her high, enthusiastic zeal should fail,
Her labor for reform would all be shent !

MRS. J. SPRATT.

THIS world a better woman does not hold
    Than Mrs. Spratt, wife of dyspeptic Jack—
(Who is, however, not quite half so black
As he's been painted!)   She's a heart of gold !
And—since I know it, though I've not been told—
I here make bold to say behind her back,
That all upon this earth she still doth lack
Of being truly sainted is a tighter hold
Upon her temper on house-cleaning days !
So raise your voice, my muse, and sing her praise !
O omniscient goddess, you have seen
How patiently she bears her husband's mean,
Dyspeptic groans and pneumogastric ways ;
And well you know she really likes the lean !

JILL.

WHEN stumbling Jack, his empty pail to fill,
    Climbs life's steep hill in search of Mimir's water,
Pray tell me why must Embla's luckless daughter,
The willful, wayward, careless smiling Jill,
When Jack falls down and all his pains doth spill,
Come falling, bawling, stumbling, sprawling 'ater?
I asked a Norn. So strongly I besought her,
She told the whole. Now listen if you will !

Jill loves her Jack. When he his crown doth crack,
She cannot bear a prudent, uncracked crown ;
So when life's hill, head-first, he tumbles down,
She needs must tumble too, hard at his back,
As you might do who live in this same town,
If you loved shambling, stumbling, crackbrained Jack.

YVETTE, THE BALLET DANCER.

HAVE you no soul at all, fair, lithe Yvette,
   Are you then, but a shameless, dancing sprite,
One of those nixies who each Friday night,
Dance with small imps until the moon has set—
With small, singed imps, smoke-stained and black as jet
Your limbs, swift-glancing and your feet so light
Bewilder foolish eyes and charm our sight
Until the harm and shame we quite forget !

Far down in Sheol, wicked nixies dance
Before gray, bald-crowned sinners and smooth boys,—
Smooth, beardless boys who dream that Sheol's joys
Shall be eternal !   How their lithe limbs glance
In the red, gleaming fire-light as they dance,
Mad with delight that ruins and destroys !

JEZEBEL.

WITH snowy arms and swelling bosom bare,
  Queen Jezebel in her high hall of state,
Feasted the brave, the noble and the great !
Bright gleamed her jewelled frontlet, and most fair
Shone on her white, curved throat a ruby rare,
Red as shed blood and glowing as the hate
Of famished slaves who stand without her gate,
Clenching their futile hands in vain despair !

Her voice is music, low and soft and sweet
As a clear viol's last sweet, echoing tone ;
But harsh and full of discord is the moan
Of piteous children, starving in the street.
Close then her gates, and let no sound unmeet
Mar the blent harmonies about her throne !

.

MAG.

SHE sits half-bent, a foul and sin-wrecked hag,
    An outcast daughter of the race of Heth !
In the last days of life ill-spent, her breath
Comes in sharp gasps.   Her shoulders sag ;
Her chapless jaws with drooling curses wag.
'' Lo, is not this (one says and shuddereth)
Incarnate Sin in love with hell and death ?''
But the small street imps call her '' Work-House Mag !''

But thou that judgest, whosoe'er thou art,
Hast thou no kinship with such souls as hers
Who do not choose their roles or know the part
The prompter gives them when the curtain stirs
And rises on a stage where still recurs
This tragedy earth's sad Christ knows by heart ?

GRETCHEN AND THE DAISY.

TEN leaves of white around a heart of gold !
  One leaf for love ; the next for bitter grief ;
One leaf for falsehood ; one for fond belief !
By ten such leaves is Gretchen's fortune told !
So much of life can one small flower unfold
To her who plucks it, leaf by fatal leaf,
(The first for joy, the last for bitter grief)
Till naught remaineth but the heart of gold !

Yea, she loved much and much is she forgiven !
Though sin brings death, love draws us ever on ;
And ever still our rough ways lead above,
Until at last for love's sake, sin is shriven.
So shall we learn when other life is gone,
There is in heaven no other life but love !

MARIA BEATIFICATA.

THAT same sad Mary who on Calvary,
    Wept with her loving heart wrung by despair,
Sits now, chief of the blessed souls who share
The secret knowledge of Gethsemane ;
The meaning of Golgotha's mystery ;
For Christ has written it in letters fair
Upon the golden Book of Life.   And there
The highest angels of eternity
Kneel and cry out " Hosannah !" to His name ;
" Hosannah !" cry the blessed cherubim ;
" Hosannah !" cry the mighty seraphim,
Crowned with their frontlets of fair, shining flame ;
" Hosannah !" all heaven's hosts cry out to Him ;
" Blessed, thrice blessed be His glorious name !"

THE HORATIAN ODE AND THE
TUSCAN SONNET.

THE HORATIAN ODE AND THE
TUSCAN SONNET.

THE earlier English sonnets were imitated from the mediæval Tuscan, but they do not adequately represent the principle of musical vowel succession from which the Tuscan sonnet derives its greatest charm.

The English sonnet-writers devoted their attention to metre, governed with rigid formality by final (end) rhymes recurring at rigidly formal intervals.

In the sonnet of Petrarch as in the best classical verse, metre is subordinated to the musical laws which determine melody.

It is hard to decide to what extent Petrarch consciously practiced these laws. It is clear that he was not master of the highly artistic system of line and staff rhyme which characterizes the lyrics of Horace, but it is almost equally certain that he and the other great Italian masters of that period had partly recovered the accent of the classical Latin, and had thus become conscious of the melody of the verse of the Augustan epoch.

All who practice music or habitually read verse aloud
know that the ear will apprehend the system governing a
melody, instrumental or vocal, long before the mind is able
to analyze it.   This is illustrated in the case of Father Prout
whose mastery of the languages of the Latin peoples, ancient
and modern, so educated his ear that in translating the
Horatian ode " Lydia, dic per omnes," he divided the
Latin throughout on the pauses which develop the internal
rhyme governing the verse.   He was almost equally suc-
cessful in scanning the melody of the ode to Leuconoe, but
he never ventured to trust his ear in a generalization which
might have made him master of the secret of the melody of
Greece and Rome.

Prout's translations of Horace are founded on his ear for
the melody of the verse as those of Bulwer-Lytton are on a
theory of the metre.   Any one who will compare Prout's
translation of the ode to Lydia with that of Lord Lytton,
will see at once how it is possible for the ear to separate
two systems which in the verse of Horace, harmonize
perfectly.   The Horatian verse is governed chiefly by
" homœoteleuton " as defined by Aristotle in his work on
rhetoric ; and approximately in the new Century dictionary.
The term is more comprehensive than the English word
rhyme, but the rhyme of the Horatian verse when it occurs

at the end of the staves of melody is exactly similar to the rhyme governing the verse of the best English writers.

Horatian verse, however, was written with a careful regard to succession of vowel tones not only at the ends of the staves of the verse but in each separate verse itself.

Horatian line rhyme follows closely the principles on which the air is composed in setting a song to the harp. This "Tonkunst" characterizes the best odes of Horace as it does the verse of Homer and the Greek poets. The single perfect example the writer can recall in English verse is the line of Coleridge :

"In Xanadu did Kubla Khan—"

"Xan" and "Khan;" "du" and "Ku;" "a" and "bla" fill the definition of perfect line rhymes, while the "i's" in "in" and in "did" are strongly assonant.

In the Horatian ode, as in Homer,* the metre of the verse

---

* In his essay on the Homeric poems, Plutarch defines two varieties of stave rhymes, the homœoteleuton and its variant, the homœoptoton, the latter word denoting the artistic adaptation of case endings, and the other ordinary rhymes and assonances of Greek syntax. The use of these varieties of rhyme under the governing influence of parison or isokolon is mainly the secret of melody in classical verse. It is of the greatest importance to remember that parison and isokolon operate generally from the beginning of verses, and are not necessarily checked by their endings. (Compare Quintilian B IX, ch. III, 75 to 85.)

regulates melody and prevents jingling. In a language like classical Latin where the **grave** accent tends always to final syllables with a stronger stress even than in modern French ; or like Greek in which (except a few particles) every syllable not otherwise accented has the grave accent, jingling would be frequent **in verse unless melody was** regulated by metre depending not only on accent but on stressing the vowels to give them musical **time. These** agencies **check what might** otherwise be the excessive **vowel assonance of** the verse and **give it a harmony which has** never been **equalled** perhaps, **since in** the classical **languages the** grave **accent** on final **syllables ceased to be** strong **enough to hold the acute in musical balance.**

The end rhymes of modern verse serve a double purpose. They show the measure of the verse, and bind together the separate verses of which the poem is composed. The stave rhymes with which the line rhymes of Horatian verse are reinforced, also serve to bind the verses together in systems or stanzas, and to define the staves of which each verse and stanza is composed. But they do not otherwise limit the verse. They may be coincident with line rhymes. They may occur at the end of verses as in English. They may and they often do, define the metre of entire verses as is so frequently the case in the dialogue of Aeschylus. But they do not severely limit the verse. Occurring at musical rather than mathematical intervals, they give the Horatian ode a freedom which modern lyrical verse has lost. An examination of the melody of the following lines written in a common English metre, will suggest some of the uses of rhyme in classical " blank verse."

" The dawn's fleet ray, a flower in the grass,
    Dew drops on the lawn, sweet scents in May ;
    The bird's soft song at morning heard—
    These shall not pass though kingdom's fall ;
    Though all else change these shall not pass ! "

Much of the art of Horatian verse consists of skilfully disguised line rhymes which are often used to rest the voice after a series of stave rhymes, as in the third verse above where the melodious antithesis between "bird" and "heard" defines the verse of which it is a part and checks the voice for an interval of melody longer than that generally punctuated by the period. Such staff rhymes as "ray" and " May;" "grass" and "pass," "fall" and "all," are also intended to punctuate the verse, mark its time and develop those words or syllables which are thought worthy of special emphasis. The Horatian stave rhyme serves all these purposes and many others, for it is nearly always at the end

of a sense-clause as well as of a bar of melody, and the
coincidence between these is a powerful aid not only to
remembering the verse but to appreciating its subtleties of
meaning.

The Horatian ode to "Pyrrha" is a very melodious
example of "homœoteleuton" in its form of line and stave
rhymes as will be seen from a close examination of the
opening lines :

> "Quis multa gracilis te puer in rosa
> Perfusus liquidis urget odoribus
> Grato, Pyrrha, sub antro?
> Cui flavam religas comam
> Simplex munditiis !" ***

The final syllables of "gracilis" "liquidis" and "mun-
ditiis" are examples of the stave rhyme, recurring at definite
musical intervals to bind the separate verses together. The
first verse gives a beautiful example of line rhymes in
"quis" and "gracilis" "multa" and "rosa" the final
syllables of which were stressed as in French except that
the pronunciation of the consonant with the subsequent
vowel as in Italian makes the grave stress stronger than on
final syllables in French prose. In the second verse "per-
fusus" and "odoribus" have terminations which give

perfect line rhymes while the " u's " and " i's " in the verse
afford musical assonances.   The governing rhymes of the
preceding ode, " To Sestius," are even more melodious.

> " Solvitur acris hyems grata vice veris et favoni,
>   Trahuntque siccas machinae carinas ;
>   Ac neque jam stabulis gaudet pecus aut arator igni ;
>   Nec prata canis albicant pruinis."

Although the almost perfect music of this verse is lost
when it is read with the accent and vowel values of the
Teutonic tongues, much of it remains when either the
French or Italian accentuation is used.   But unfortunately
the French vowels represent a different musical key, while
in Italian though the key is the same or almost the same,
the shifting of accent away from final syllables disguises
the true nature of the verse.

Almost obscured in modern verse, the classical principle
of melody survives to a much greater extent in musical
composition.   In the best German and Scotch instrumental
melodies, it is easy to find entire systems, governed by the
same laws which govern the lyrics of Homer and Horace
and so closely analagous to them as to be scientifically
correspondent.   It is worthy of special note that this is
most apt to be true of those airs which have taken the
greatest hold on the memory of the people.

A fact which might otherwise seem incredible admits of
very simple explanation. The most artistic classical writers
including those of the Augustan age were governed largely
by the system of melody which governs the Homeric verse
—which the Homeric verse develops as a race-inheritance,
originating in an antiquity as remote as the origin of
language. The Homeric verse is truly lyrical. In its vowel
succession and governing rhymes, it corresponds with the
music of the lyre to which it was intoned.

It is obviously difficult for any one who has a good voice
and an accurate ear for musical tone and time, to depart far
from the tone and time of the musical instrument to which
he sings or recites in extemporaneous composition. The
voice and the instrument affect each other mutually in the
rhapsody or extemporaneous lyric—a fact which goes far to
account for the superior melody of the Homeric rhapsodies
and of all other genuine improvisations to music.

The laws governing the educated human ear are such
that it is certain as anything can be scientifically, that the
Homeric verse, in its tone and time is the analogue of the
Greek music of its day. The question of pitch and its con-
nection with accent in classical verse need not be considered
here, though the review of what some classical writers have
said on the subject, might be read with advantage as
Rousseau has given it in his musical dictionary.

A comparatively close idea of the melody of Homeric verse may be gained by any musician who will analyze the melody of Schubert's "Hark, Hark, the Lark!" as it would be played on a harp of a single octave, with the pauses in the music governed by those of the verse to which it is set, thus:

E   F   B   B   B   D   C   C
Hark, hark the lark at heaven's gate sings
G   G G   Ga   G   C
And Phœbus gins to rise'
E   F   B   B   B C   E   G
His steeds to water at those springs
G   G G   G A   G   E
On chaliced flowers that lies.

The principles of time, tone, and pitch, governing the execution of this melody on any instrument or by the voice, are dominated by a higher principle which governed in the mind of the composer—that of melodious antithesis, under which like sounds are set against each other in musical equipoise. It was for this purpose that the so-called "homœoteleuton" was chiefly used in classical composition as end rhymes are used in English verse. Only a great poet, however, and one thoroughly master of the underlying

simplicities of vowel harmony could venture such a vowel
succession as that of the repeated " G " notes character-
izing the melody of the second and fourth antithetical
periods in this quatrain.   Homer does it frequently in
verse that expresses elevated feeling, and Horace imitates
him in it though with caution, and of course not with the
same success in a language which lacked the grave musical
qualities of the Greek.

The fundamental law of melodious antithesis is that like
sounds with a difference must recur at musical intervals.
Thus in Schubert's air above " C–C " at the end of the
first antithetical period, and " G–C " at the end of the
second are like sounds differentiated—to make melody, in
the first place, and in the second to measure the music so
that the ear can grasp its rhythm.   Again, the C at the end
of the second antithetical period blends with the E at the
beginning of the next to form a melodious correspondence
with the " G–E " at the end of the fourth.   Such corres-
pondences as this are classed by Aristotle under the general
heading of " paromœosis " a word which may mean alliter-
ation, assonance, consonance and rhyme.   As all assonances, consonances and alliterations are rhymes when they
are perfect, it may be said for the sake of illustrating the
analogy between vocal and instrumental melody that the

recurrence of like sounds with a difference in the air from Schubert constitutes rhyme, and that in instrumental melody rhymes serve the same purpose they do in vocal.

This purpose is recognized by Aristotle who writes in concluding the ninth chapter of his third book on rhetoric, that "it is possible for the same example (in Greek prose) to be both an antithesis equipoised and having rhyme." (Bohn translation of 1890, page 234.)

This use of rhyme in the prose writing of the Greeks and Romans was carried to what some condemned as an excess. Quintillian* does not so condemn it, but Aulus Gellius (XVII—8) has preserved a fragment from the fifth satire of Lucilius in which it is severely attacked. No doubt the ear of the poet objected to a recurrence of rhymes which so easily becomes a jingle where it is not governed by a correct sense of melody.

Unless verse written under classical laws is thus governed, it becomes discordant and disagreeable. The disuse of the lyre in composition and recitation left the ear without proper means of education, and the attempt to compose either prose or verse under the laws illustrated in the odes

---

*Confer Quintillian IX Book, chapter III, 75 to 87. English translations of the technical terms of classical literary art are frequently inadequate and misleading.

of Horace as they are to some extent in the prose of Cicero,
necessarily resulted in artificiality and discord.

The governing influence of rhyme in determining melody
in what may be called the Augustan age of Norse poetry, is
noticed by Messrs. Vigfusson and Powell in their Corpus
Poeticum Boreale, from which this may be quoted :

"There are two kinds of rhyme or sound-echo used in
the later Northern metres—*full rhyme* which may be single
as 'take' and 'bake' or *double* as 'taking' and 'baking;'
consonant rhyme or consonance as 'take' and 'cook.'

Rhymes may be *end rhymes* coming at the end of each
half line or line of a set ; or they may be *line rhymes*,
coming both within one-half line.   Line rhymes may come
within any syllable of a word."

This is strongly suggestive of the system governing
classical verse as it is illustrated in Homer and Horace,
whose rhymes, however, are nearly always perfect as in the
very best modern poetry.   Their recurrence as stave rhymes
in consonance with the line rhymes of single verses not
only marks the rhythmical bars of the verse, but defines its
sense-clauses in a way which often elucidates passages not
readily intelligible otherwise.   The fact that the pauses in
Latin and Greek are so different from those of any modern
positional language is one of the factors which combine

to make it difficult to recognize the melody of classical verse. The first step towards regaining it for educational purposes must be the repunctuation of classical texts in harmony with those conversational pauses by which the syntactical agreements of the language, depending on its agreements of termination, were developed so that the ear could readily grasp them—as of course it could not have done otherwise. Even if we could speak Greek or Latin now with the accent and alphabetical values of the first century before Christ, an Athenian or Roman of that period would probably have great difficulty in understanding us because the pauses used in modern positional languages tend to obscure completely the relations and agreements of the words in a Greek or Latin sentence.

Of course these relations were soon obscured by the shifting of accent. When the grave accent lost its governing value, the composition of verse under classical laws became merely a matter of pedantry. The staff rhyme of classical verse must have assimilated with the rhymes of religious and popular "proses" to make the system which comes down to us in the earlier proses of the Christian church— a system which is well illustrated in the "Stabat Mater" and "Dies Irae." Such proses, it may be asserted with positiveness, constituted the beginning of the modern system of verse as it appears in the earlier Tuscan sonnets

and ballatas, in the verse of the Northern minnesingers
and troubadors, and more rudely in the popular heroic
ballads of England and Scotland.

This, however, was not the earliest form of the proses
or chants used in the Christian church. In their earlier
form, the rhymes and assonances which govern them and
determine their melody are free and much more melodious
than it is possible for rhymes and assonances to be when
mathematically fixed at rigid intervals apart. Perhaps one
of the most beautiful proses in existence, if indeed it is
not the most perfect example of vowel harmony in religious
poetry is the chant in the book of Revelations beginning
"And I saw a new heaven and a new earth." Although it
might have been pronounced rude by a rhetorician of that
day accustomed to the niceties of melodious antithesis in
the artificial style of the later oratorical writers, it shows
that the writer was familiar with the leading rules of com-
positions commonly taught in the schools by students of
Homer, and that he had an ear for the melody of language
hardly equalled by that of Homer himself. The book of
Revelations is characterized by the frequent recurrence of
such rhapsodies, and they are invaluable as illustrations
of the beginnings of modern religious melody.

In the time of Petrarch, the criticism which has its highest
reach in the counting of syllables had not yet begun to

dominate the composition of verse. With Petrarch as with Horace and Homer, melody was the supreme force. His verse was confined by end rhymes, it is true, but he did not allow these to master him. He had no hesitation in using fifteen or more syllables in a sonnet line, and as many accents as he saw fit. His line rhymes which determine the measure of his melody, are highly musical but not systematic as are those of the best classical odes. His staff rhymes which occur frequently have the appearance of being the result of unconscious musical suggestion while it is only possible for ignorance of the nature of classical verse to question the art with which its rhyming syllables are arranged. This art, developed by the very nature of the languages of which it is a part, appears in Petrarch in his mastery of the principles of harmonious vowel succession. His verse resembles that of Horace in that the vowels are played upon as if they were the strings of the harp or the keys of a piano. This is an art which is still possible for English verse. It may finally become possible also for English versifiers to do as Petrarch and Horace have done in subjecting rhythm to the laws of melody. If an anapestic stave suits Petrarch better than an iambic, he uses it with the same freedom he shows in extending or shortening his verses to suit the demands of his melody. His ear taught him that the reading of verse by a fixed scheme of rhythm,

depending on the recurrence of sounds of the same length
at the same or nearly the **same** intervals throughout lyrics
or longer poems would result in **such droning** as characterizes the hexameters of that great scholar and critic Voss,
whose German "hexameter" version of the Homeric poems
has influenced for the worse not only American prosodists
but even American writers of verse.   It is doubtful if there
is in Homer a single period of five lines which can be read
successfully by the hexameter of Voss, even **when the effect
of** the grave accent in Greek is lost sight of *   **It may be**
asserted with confidence that there are no two periods of ten
lines each **in** Homer in which **the pauses** governing **the**
verse repeat each other ; and **it is equally safe** to say that
the pauses which govern Horatian **verse do not permit** it
to be read by any metrical scheme under which the attempt
is made to reduce every verse and stanza to the fixed rule
of every other verse and stanza in the same ode.   No verse
is more artistic than that of Horace, and while it is not as
free as that of Homer, it is freer than **that of Burns.**   Its
metre is not **the shackle of the galley-slave** but the rudder
of the galley, cutting the **waters of the** Aegean when
"**sharp winter melts in** change of spring **and** west winds,
blowing, swell whitening **sails upon blue, sunlit seas.**"

* In scholia B on Hephaiston of Alexandria, the seven varieties of
heroic verse used in the Homeric poems are defined and illustrated.
Both the scholiae and the text of Hephaiston deserve careful study.